Hallows Eve

TIME PATROL

Cool Gus Publishing

http://coolgus.com

This is a work of fiction. Names, characters, places, and incidents either are the product of the author's imagination or are used fictitiously, and any resemblance to actual persons living or dead, business establishments, events, or locales is entirely coincidental.

Hallows Eve (Time Patrol) by Bob Mayer
COPYRIGHT © 2017 by Bob Mayer

ISBN: 978-1621253129

Hallows Eve

TIME PATROL

BOB MAYER

"I'm not superstitious. I'm a witch. Witches aren't superstitious. We are what people are superstitious of." Terry Pratchett

Dedication

For
Nancy Debra Cavanaugh

Where The Time Patrol Ended Up This Particular Day: 31 October

! ! ! Attention government sponsors of cyber warfare and those who profit from it ! ! !

Beginning of Patebin Page of the Shadow Brokers
ZERO DAY; ZERO YEAR

The Gunman shot the guy in the Fedex outfit in the left eye. The slice of pizza Fedex man had been holding hit the floor with a splat. He slumped in the seat, dead before he was aware he was going to die.

"No double-tap?" Ivar asked, trying to remain calm.

"No need, as you can clearly see."

"Right. I was taught double-tap."

"You were taught correctly," Gunman said, "but situations differ." He waggled the gun, which was now pointed at Ivar. "Twenty-two High Standard. A classic. One shot, eyeball, is enough. But you must be very accurate. The eye socket is a small target."

"Right." Ivar swallowed. "And now?"

It is Now. Zero Day in Zero Year. How we got to be here via the computer timeline?

1801: Joseph Marie invents a loom using wood punch cards to weave certain fabric designs, the forerunner of computer punch cards.

1822: Charles Babbage conceptualizes a calculator powered by steam and is funded by the British Government, but his project fails.

1890: Herman Hollerith designs a punch system, not a machine, to help calculate the 1880 census and accomplishes the task in only three years (done by hand it took seven); the company he starts will eventually be known as IBM.

1936: Alan Turing conceptualizes a 'universal machine' that would be capable of computing anything that is computable, which is the essence of a computer. Sort of.

"'And now'?" The Gunman seemed to realize something. "Excuse me. I have failed to introduce myself. I am Victor."

"'Victor'?" Ivar nodded. "Sure. Victor. I'm Ivar."

Some things change; some don't.

"You are not my contact," Victor said, "but I strongly suspect you are involved in this matter."

"What matter is that?" Ivar asked.

"We had an incident a while back. In the Negev."

This was worse than the mob, Ivar realized. *The fraking Israelis.*

"Someone appeared," Victor said. "Like you did. Caused great damage. I read the report and watched the surveillance tapes." He pointed the pistol with the stubby suppressor directly at Ivar's left eye. "Who are you and how did you get here?"

"Up! Children of Zulu, your day has come. Up! And destroy them all." Shaka Zulu

Zululand, Africa, 31 October 1828 A.D.

"If you have no more prophecies," Shaka said, "you have no more time."

"But, my King!" the old woman protested. "My words were true!"

"That means you are a true witch," Shaka reasoned. "And should die."

Shaka slammed the *ikhwa* into the old woman's chest, pinning her to the ground.

"Come here, spy," Shaka said, gesturing for Eagle to approach his throne composed of human bones. "There is something I want to show you. Perhaps in your treasonous life, you have seen something like it."

Eagle knew he stood no chance against Shaka, *iklwa* to *iklwa*, regardless of the Naga blade on his own. He walked forward, skirting around the dead woman.

Shaka lifted something heavy and tossed it toward Eagle. It thudded and rolled once.

It is 1828 A.D. Russia declares war on Turkey in support of Greek independence; Shaka Zulu, the most powerful Zulu ruler, dies (maybe); South Carolina declares the right of states to nullify Federal law which will have consequences in a couple of decades; a storm off of Gibraltar sinks over 100 ships; Noah Webster publishes the first American dictionary; Simon Bolivar becomes dictator of Venezuela; Andrew Jackson is elected the seventh President of the United States with 642,553 votes after having not been named President in the 1824 election despite receiving the most electoral votes.

"What is that?" Shaka demanded.

Eagle knew why he was here.

Some things change; some don't.

"That, great King, is the head of a mighty beast we call a Grendel. And if there is one, there is at least one more like it. Larger, more dangerous. Capable of giving birth to many, many more."

Shaka laughed, a jagged edge to it. "At least *one* more? As the witch prophesized, in the Valley of Death to the west. There are dozens of these beasts, guarding a watering hole. It was a mighty fight to get this one head. They were sent here to torment me in my grief."

"Until an hour before the Devil fell, God thought him beautiful in Heaven."
Arthur Miller, *The Crucible*
Salem Massachusetts, 31 October 1692 A.D.

"I really thought—" Pandora began, but she paused, cocking her head. "Do you have the Sight?" Her voice was lower, almost a whisper.

"Sort of," Lara said.

"Do you sense him?"

Lara *did* sense something or someone. In the forest. Moving. Coming this way. She'd felt this presence before; even met it.

"Joey," she whispered.

"Who is Joey?" Pandora said, turning in the direction of the presence, lifting her Naga to the ready. "You met one before?"

"He is darkness," Lara said. "Evil."

It is 1692 A.D. The world's population is roughly 710 million with 436 million of those in Asia; Diego de Vargas, and Spanish colonists, retake Santa Fe, New Mexico from the Pueblo people after 12 years of exile and the event is still celebrated in the city; in February, the first people are accused of witchcraft in Salem: Sarah Good, Sarah Osborne, and Tituba; an earthquake devastates Jamaica and the resulting tsunami kills two to three thousand and destroys the capital, Port Royal; a Chinese Emperor issues the Edict of Toleration, recognizing all Roman Catholic priests (not just Jesuits) and legalizing their right to convert Chinese; on June 10th the first to be hanged in Salem is Bridget Bishop.

"You do have some Sight," Pandora acknowledged. "It is Legion." She lowered the point of her Naga staff slightly. "It is going away. But it knows we're here."

Some things change; some don't.

"Why didn't he attack?" Lara asked. She had sensed more than just the Legion. There were more things out there. Not human.

"It is not here for us," Pandora said.

"Who is he here for? And why are you calling him 'it'?"

"I truly expected it to be Scout that was chosen for this mission," Pandora said.

"Why is that?" Lara asked.

"Because if you fail in this mission, Scout will cease to exist."

"I am alive today. I may not be here tomorrow."
Indira Gandhi (on 30 October, the night before her assassination)
New Delhi, 31 October 1984 A.D.

"I am Indira. And you are?"

"Neeley, Prime Minister."

"There is no need to be formal, is there?" Gandhi asked. "Not now. Not this evening, actually very early morning as the hour has already passed midnight into a new day."

"Yes ma'am," Neeley said, a cup of tea cooling on the table in front of her, while the Prime Minister of India took a sip from her own. A gun rested on Neeley's lap, hidden by the tablecloth.

"Indira, please. And is Neeley your first name or surname?"

"It's just my name."

"Curious. Surely you were born with a full name?"

"I was."

Gandhi held up a hand. "I sense the issue is one that is sensitive to you. Forgive my intrusion. Neeley. Most interesting. You sound American, but there is a trace of an accent in your English. Having grown up here but being schooled in Europe, I have heard many voices. A bit of French perhaps?"

"I lived there for a while," Neeley admitted.

"Ah, France," Gandhi said. "Joan d'Arc. A true hero. A woman ahead of her time."

It is 1984 A.D. Cirque Du Soleil is founded; a 19 year old goes into a deep coma after an auto accident—he'll come out of it in 2003; Vanessa Williams becomes the first African-American to become Miss America, but it doesn't last; the IRA attempts to assassinate Prime Minister Thatcher and the British Cabinet with a bomb; Galileo is formally forgiven by the Vatican for his correct theory on the Earth's orbit, a bit late for him; Ronald Reagan is elected President; Apple introduces the Mac with an iconic commercial; the Winter Olympics are held in Sarajevo; crack cocaine is introduced in Los Angeles; Chrysler introduces the first mini-van (yay?); Iran accuses Iraq of using chemical weapons.

Gandhi looked down. "And you brought a gun."

Neeley put the pistol on the table. "For protection."

Some things change. Some don't.

"Really? And you know how to use it?"

"I do."

Gandhi took a sip of tea, reminding Neeley of her own.

She picked up the cup and sampled. "This is very nice."

"My own mixture," Gandhi said. "Tea is such a strange symbol in my country. The British exploited us for it but it is still a rich export that helps drive our economy. It seems everything in life cuts both ways. Now we no longer have the British but we still have our tea."

Neeley was never one for small talk so she didn't say anything.

Gandhi indicated the pistol. "Will you shoot me with that?"

"Have you heard of a ship called the good Reuben James
Manned by hard fighting men both of honor and fame?"

5

Woody Guthrie
The North Atlantic, 31 October 1941 A.D.

"Who are you?" the man hissed, leaning close, putting pressure on the blade at Roland's neck.

"Roland."

"Are you friend or foe?"

Roland slowly moved his left hand toward the handle of his dagger. "Friend or foe of who?" Roland asked as the destroyer *USS Reuben James* rolled steeply, a North Atlantic wave tossing the four-stack destroyer.

"I was told one out of time would come," the man said. "I felt the disturbance of your arrival. Why are you here?"

Roland answered as carefully, and vaguely, as he could, which wasn't hard for him. "To make sure everything happens as it should."

It is 1941 A.D. Elmer's Pet Rabbit, aka Bugs Bunny, premiers; FDR is sworn in for his third term as President; all persons born in Puerto Rico henceforth will be U.S. Citizens; Grand Coulee Dam begins to generate electricity; Citizen Kane premiers; Z3, the world's first working programmable automatic computer is introduced in Berlin; Joe DiMaggio begins his 56 game hitting streak; the first major airborne assault in history is launched by the Germans on Crete; Goring directs Heydrich to draw up plans for the Final Solution with Himmler to be in charge; the first Jeep rolls off the production line; the T4 program is initiated by the Nazis, euthanizing people with disabilities; Jews in the occupied territories must wear a Star of David; construction of the Pentagon building begins; German troops can see the steeples of Moscow, much as Napoleon had a century before, but it's snowing and cold, much like Napoleon experienced; Hong Kong falls to the Japanese; a breakfast called Cheerios is released.

The man laughed without mirth. "What *should* happen? You know? What do you know?"

"This ship sinks."

Some things change; some don't.

"*This* ship sinks'?" The man was incredulous. "Who cares about *this* ship? It's the other ship, the submarine that we have to worry about. *That's* the one we have to destroy."

"Every man must do two things alone; he must do his own believing and his own dying."
Martin Luther
Wittenberg, Germany, 31 October 1517 A.D.

Legion put one blade to his lips and licked it. "Your blood is indeed sweet. Are you a virgin?"

"Are you serious?" Scout said. "I think—" and she darted to her right, jumping onto a pew, and continuing high into the air.

No one ever looks up, Nada had always preached.

It is 1517 A.D. The Ottoman Empire captures Cairo, deposing the Mamluk Sultanate; the first official diplomatic mission of a European country to China is made in Hong Kong; the 1st Duke of Suffolk is born; Pope Leo X signs the 5th Council of Lateran covering such things as the Church allowing pawn shops to give loans to the poor.

Of course, the move was worthless given Legion was watching her. But her focus on time was everything and the world was slowing down once more. She could feel the wood under her sandal, her muscles contracting, expanding, pushing her up. She twisted as she went up, aware of the air brushing against her skin, the musty odor of the church, and most of all, Legion turning, bringing one blade up to parry, the other ready to thrust upward and gut her.

Some things change; some don't.

But he was too slow as the tip of Scout's Naga dagger drew a thin red line along the side of his scalp starting at the temple, slicing through his ear, and ending at the back of the neck.

Scout landed on her feet, unscathed. "That was pretty cool. Didn't know I could do that."

7

But *BEFORE* the Ides of March and *AFTER* they came back from Valentines Day

The Possibility Palace
Where? Can't tell you. When? Can't tell you.

Lara stood on the edge of the Pit, staring aimlessly into its depths. She closed her eyes, letting go off her surroundings and opened her mind to the world and more than the world:

They grieve their teammate.

Would they grieve me the same?

Selfish much?

Scout would. She has a good heart. Moms, too. Roland is an odd duck, but he'd eat nails for Moms. And for Scout. Frak. He'd give his all for any member of the team. Probably even me. He's got a weird thing about females. Mother issues, probably.

Eagle would too. Even Ivar, weird as he is.

Doc gave all.

But I didn't. Give all. I couldn't go through that door. Face the truth of my past, of whatever, and whoever, I might be.

So Doc died.

They grieve, but I stand here alone, in my pity party.

I don't like this. All these voices in the Pit. Billions of people. A pulsing, throbbing mass of—I don't know what to call what it is I hear/feel.

Existence?

So many regrets echo out of the past. Out of death.

Do they have a place in the universe. Did they matter? The billions and billions who've gone before?

But the team.

They're alive and they're grateful. In their grief, what they don't speak out loud is gratitude that they are still alive. That the one they grieve is someone else.

That is the human condition.

Who speaks for the dead?

This fraking Pit. Billions of them trying to be heard and drowning each other out.

But Scout's song came through clear from the team room behind me:

'Hold me in your thoughts.

Take me to your dreams.'

She grieves a lot for a kid.

Kid?

She's older than I am.

I think.

She'd go with me through that door in my dream.

But I could never take her there.

'Here there be monsters!'

Frak me! Who was that? Where did that come from?

Who spoke that?

If there be monsters, bring them on!

"You all right?" Scout was right behind Lara.

"I heard something," Lara said, opening her eyes, returning to this world, bound by three dimensions, while time moved in a single linear direction.

Scout looked concerned, a strangely comforting thing for Lara. "What did you hear?"

"A voice. Someone calling out."

"In the debrief you said you heard us singing, coming out of the Pit," Scout said. "Like that?"

"Sort of," Lara agreed. "But not the team. Someone else. And not a song."

9

"Who?" Scout asked.

"I don't know."

"Man or woman?"

"Man."

"What did the voice say?"

"'Here there be monsters'," Lara said.

Scout nodded as if that made perfect sense. "Yeah. Old maps used to put that in the blank spaces that hadn't been explored yet. Eagle talked about it when Roland went back to 999." Scout reached up and gently touched the bandage on Lara's cheek. "Does it hurt?"

"A little."

Scout flushed. "Stupid question. You were cut. Of course it hurts. You don't want me poking around." She put her arm through Lara's. "Come on. Moms wants you in the team room. There's something we have to do."

"Shouldn't she be in a hospital?" Lara asked as Scout led her along the spiral ramp around the edge of the Pit. It descended into all of known history, a record of this timeline.

"Dane had one of his people patch her up. But I don't think she's going dancing any time soon."

Lara laughed. "I can't see Moms dancing."

"You should have seen her in a tennis outfit," Scout said. "She can actually look really nice if she tries. She looked pretty good on the last mission."

"She always serious," Lara said as they reached the door of the team room.

"She's responsible." Scout opened the door.

Moms was in a wheelchair, one leg heavily bandaged and stretched out straight. She looked like she belonged outdoors, with wide shoulders, a narrow waist, and short, graying hair. Her face was weathered and there were more lines there than before.

Eagle sat on one side, Roland on the other. Ivar was across the table, his usual morose self.

"Please sit down, Lara," Moms said. "We have a tradition that dates back to our time in the Nightstalkers. How long they did it, I don't know. They were doing it when I joined and—" she paused as a realization struck her. "I guess that makes me senior on the team, since none of you were there when I arrived. Eagle," she nodded at the team sergeant, a black man with a shaved head, one side of it scarred from an IED explosion, "is next senior in terms of time on the team. And now we're the Time Patrol. But I believe strongly that traditions are important. I expect this tradition to be upheld after I'm gone."

"Of course," Eagle said, and the other four nodded.

"We take care of our own," Moms said.

She reached out. Eagle took one hand, Roland the other. The circle continued with Roland to Scout to Lara to Ivar and back to Eagle.

Moms spoke. "It is Protocol for us to acknowledge the death of a team member because no one else will. We must pay our respect and give honors. We must remember."

She nodded her head toward one of the names carved in the wood table top. MAC. "He was named Mac by the team, but regained his name and his past with his death. Sergeant First Class Eric Bowen, U.S. Army Special Forces, MOS Eighteen-Charlie, Special Forces Engineer, from Texas. We speak his rank and his name as it was."

They all spoke together: "Sergeant First Class Eric Bowen."

Moms turned her head. "Scout?"

Scout swallowed. "He was named Nada by the team," she said, "but in death he got back his name and his past and his daughter. Sergeant Major Edward Moreno, US Army Infantry and then Special Forces, Delta Force and Nightstalker. Team Sergeant. Friend. We speak his rank and his name as it was."

The team said: "Sergeant Major Edward Moreno."

"And now," Moms said, "we add another name. He was named Doc by the team, but in death gets back his name and his past. Doctor Himmat Ghatar, owner of four PhDs. We sometimes made fun of him because of that, but his knowledge saved lives. He came to the Nightstalkers from DARPA, always wanting to learn more. To know more. To understand the world around him, even though it often didn't make sense on Nightstalker's missions and even less so in the Time Patrol.

"But, like the rest of us, when given the Choice to go back and change something, or be a member of the Patrol, he chose to move forward. It cost him his life. He sacrificed himself for us in Chicago. Everyone in this room owes him their life."

Lara shifted uncomfortably, unseen by the rest but felt by Scout and Ivar.

Moms paused and the room was completely silent, until she spoke again.

"Nada and I used to talk; hard as it to believe for those of you who knew both of us. We'd seen some strange things in the Nightstalkers, to say the least. He wondered sometimes if there was something more. Something beyond this life. He always felt he had screwed his life up. Driven his family off. That guilt is part of why he chose to go back and right a wrong. He did that and more, saving the life of one of our teammates we thought had been lost." Moms glanced at Lara. "We know the dead have voices. Lara can hear them in the Pit."

Lara shifted. Scout squeezed her hand.

"What that means," Moms continued, "I don't know. Are these voices she hears real? Do the dead exist somewhere else? Is there another level of existence beyond this one?

"Now we know there are Fates. There are other timelines. There is a Shadow. But there is so much out there we *don't* know. So I like to think there is a higher plane of existence for people like Mac and Nada and Doc. Where they are rewarded for their sacrifices in this existence in which we struggle and fight. There has to be something better."

Moms nodded at Eagle to continue.

"Doc left no immediate family," Eagle said. "His body is wherever things go when a bubble collapses. He will have no grave in Arlington. He will only have his name in this table top once I carve it."

"All we can do is keep him in our hearts," Scout said.

"In our hearts," the rest of the team, except, Lara, murmured.

*****

Dane acknowledged Frasier with a slight nod when the Time Patrol psychologist entered his office. The Time Patrol administrator was going through a stack of folders.

"Personnel records?" Frasier asked. "Recruits?"

"We're below minimum operating strength," Dane said. "Moms' wound is going to sideline her for a while. If we get an alert for another mission, we're in trouble."

"There might not be time to train an outside candidate adequately," Frasier said. "We need someone with Special Ops experience. An operator we can get up to speed quickly."

"Is that your professional opinion?" Dane asked.

Frasier bristled. "I'm here to do a job. If you don't want me here, I'll be glad to leave."

Dane put down the folder he'd been perusing and pulled his reading glasses down on his nose so he could peer over them. "That's the kind of statement that causes me to give you grief. Stating the obvious. You know there's no walking away from the Time Patrol. You're in it for life. Or death, whichever is the case."

"You going to send Roland after me?" Frasier asked.

"No." Dane shook his head. "My apologies. I just don't like recent events. We were lucky on Valentines Day. We knew something was off about that mission, but we didn't even consider what did happen."

Dane tapped the pile of folders. "I've ordered Eagle to link up with Colonel Orlando and test some recruits. Get the pipeline filled."

"Orlando is a drunk," Frasier said.

"We all know that."

"Why don't you put me in charge of recruitment?"

"Because," Dane said, "you have other responsibilities. What have you turned up regarding Lara?"

"Nothing more," Frasier said.

Dane frowned. "Really? She just came out of nowhere and appeared on that Russian plane?"

"If we believe Orlando's story."

"Eagle was with him," Dane said. "Should I doubt what Eagle said, too?"

"No. Of course not."

"What about Neeley for the team?" Dane asked. "She knows about the Time Patrol. She's even been here in the Palace. Why shouldn't we bring her on board? She's got the training and covert experience. She's very efficient. In a way, she's already been on a mission, except she's not aware of it."

"You suggested her once before," Frasier said "and I was against it. I think her relationship with Roland could cause problems."

"Roland is steady," Dane said. "So is Neeley. Expediency will have to rule on this. Even if Eagle and Colonel Orlando bring recruits into the pipeline immediately, the training will take a while."

"How about bumping someone up from the new Nightstalkers and—"

"No," Dane said. "We want to keep those two units completely separate for now. The Nightstalkers need to build cohesion." He tapped the stack of folders. "There are plenty of good people in the covert world we can check out and Orlando is going to test these." He tapped the pile of folders. "Neeley will be a good stopgap. The thing is, though, once she's in the Patrol, she stays in the Patrol. And I'd have to clear it with Hannah. She might not be thrilled with the idea of losing her best asset."

"And best friend," Frasier added.

Dane nodded. "True. And, Neeley will have to be given the Choice."

An Island Off The Coast Of Puerto Rico

At the moment, the subject of discussion, Neeley, was watching Roland try to vacation.

It was pretty futile. They were lying side by side on a beach in a secure location where people like them went to vacation and not have to worry about getting sniped, or blown up, or otherwise have a sour ending.

At the moment, they had the beach to themselves.

Seemed not many people in the covert, top secret world went on vacation.

"Would it make you feel any better if I told you we were here on a mission?" Neeley asked.

Roland perked up. "We gotta sanction someone for Hannah?" He sat up, looking around. Roland's body was a piece of art: six and a half feet of sculpted muscle. The only thing marring the image were the scars, witnesses to numerous deployments and missions. The barbwire tattoo on his forehead, which covered an old scar, furrowed as he didn't see anyone he could kill in the next few seconds.

"No," Neeley said. "But pretend we do. It will allow you to enjoy the moment."

Roland didn't do pretend well either. "At least they have a range here. And the weight room is tops."

"Of course," Neeley said. "But you've barely gone in the water and we're on a beach."

Roland frowned. "I don't like the water."

"It's not cold," Neeley said.

Roland's voice turned stubborn. "I just don't like it."

There was an edge to Roland's voice which Neeley had never heard before.

"Okay." She turned to lie on her side, facing Roland. She was six inches shorter, and long and lean where he was long and bulk. Her hair was jet black, no sign of grey. The worry lines around her eyes could use some Botox but Neeley would no more allow someone with a needle near her face, as Roland would go splash in the surf. She ran her fingers over his chest feeling flesh and scars. "Life is not a mission, Roland."

He sighed. "I know. I just never took time off before. Not really. Even on leave there had to be a place to get to, something to do. A mountain to climb or something." Others might have said that last sentence figuratively but it was literal for Roland. The two of them had taken out a pair of rogue CIA agents during a mountain climbing trip while supposedly on 'leave'. An unsanctioned mission until Hannah had retroactively sanctioned it; accepting the fact one cannot bring the dead back to life; it appeared the Fates had different powers according to Ivar from his Vicksburg mission.

And the agents *had* committed treason by betraying an op Neeley had been on. Thus Hannah, and Neeley would never give it another thought. Roland hadn't given it a thought beforehand, except how to do it.

The small island was somewhere off of Puerto Rico. On maps and Google Earth it was marked as off limits because of unexploded ordnance due to decades of being a target for naval bombardment. Buoys with warning signs were positioned all about to ward off the curious. Security was inside the buoys on swift boats to stop the stupid curious who ignored warnings.

The island *had* been a target for many years and further down the beach in either direction, and inland past the small, well camouflaged, resort, there was more than enough ordnance that hadn't gone off on impact to make any sensible person think twice, or thrice, before trying to work their way through, or never again if they did try.

"You never had me at your side before when you tried to take time off," Neeley noted.

Roland grinned, pure happiness. "Yeah." He wrapped her in his arms and she surrendered to the embrace, something she thought she'd never do again after—

That sad memory was interrupted by Neeley's Satphone buzzing.

"I don't have to answer that," she said.

"Of course you have to answer that," Roland said, regretfully letting go. "The only person who calls you is Hannah." He raised an eyebrow. "Maybe we can do a Sanction together?"

Neeley sighed and dug the phone out her bag, pushing aside a pistol, a case holding a poisoned syringe, and a clutch of throwing knives.

She activated the phone. "I'm on vacation."

"I know," Hannah said. "I'm very sorry to have interrupted but I have to ask you something."

The uncertainty in Hannah's voice made Neeley sit up.

Roland watched her, appreciating the six-pack in her abs as she did so. He was a simple man, like most men, but simple in a very honest way with women, unlike most men. A big reason Neeley was here with him.

"What is it?" Neeley asked.

"I just had a short talk with Dane," Hannah said. Her voice was slightly distorted, the result of frequency hopping and scrambling.

"Yes?"

"He wants you."

Neeley automatically looked down at Roland, who was puppy-eyeing her, with a bit more than just puppy love in the look. Roland had definitely not been neutered.

"Temporary?" Neeley asked.

"There is no temporary in that assignment," Hannah said.

"How do you feel about it?"

There was a long pause, so long that Neeley spoke again. "Are you there?"

"I'm here, Neeley." A scrambled sigh was still a sigh. "I don't want you to go. Of course."

"All right. Then I won't."

"It's *your* choice, not mine. You've got more to consider than I do. It's *your* future. It's a very different sort of unit. And mission. As you know."

"It is," Neeley said. She'd been to the Possibility Palace once, to retrieve a message for Hannah. A prediction, they'd been told. But when Hannah had opened it in the Cellar, the scroll had been blank.

"And then there's—" Hannah paused. "There's Roland to consider. Serving alongside someone you have feelings for, well . . ."

"I've done it before," Neeley said.

"You and Gant were different," Hannah said.

"We were," Neeley acknowledged. "But we did quite a few ops in our time. And Roland and I have worked together."

Roland's puppy-dog look was shifting to a frown, hearing only her side of the conversation. A different person might have pretended not to listen, but, as noted, Roland didn't do pretend well. It wasn't an intrusion on his part. He was just worried for her.

"The thing is," Hannah said, "that there's more to being part of the Time Patrol than simply signing on. They give you a choice."

"You've already told me the choice," Neeley said.

"No," Hannah said. "Even if you agree to join the Patrol, Dane said there's another choice you're going to have to make before they accept you on the team. A very serious one."

"What did he mean?"

"No clue," Hannah said. "But I didn't like it. He made it sound rather ominous. A choice with a capital C."

The word 'ominous' coming from a woman who held the power of judge, jury and executioner over every member of the covert world was disconcerting.

"You could ask Roland," Hannah continued. "I don't know if he can tell you. But he had to have made this Choice Dane is speaking of."

Neeley looked down at Roland. "I'll do that. But, really, Hannah, I don't know. I have to think about it."

"Certainly." There was another long pause. "Will you let me know when you make a decision?"

"Of course."

"Thank you. Enjoy the rest of your vacation. I'm sorry to have intruded."

"It's all right."

"No, it's not. Take care."

The phone went dead.

"What?" Roland asked.

"Dane wants me on the Time Patrol."

Roland couldn't hide his feelings. He smiled, then the smile faded to a frown. "What do you want to do?"

"I don't know. Hannah said there's some sort of 'Choice' I have to make, even if I do decide to join the team? She didn't know what it was, just that Dane sort of warned her about it."

The frown deepened on Roland's forehead. "Yeah. The Choice."

Neeley waited.

Roland sat up next to her and looked out at the ocean. "I don't know if I can tell you."

"I've been invited to join the team, Roland."

"I know. But." He thought about it. "No one said it was secret or nothing. It's just something we don't talk about on the team. No one's ever said what their Choice was. Except Nada. We all know what Nada's was, cause he chose to go back."

"'Go back'?"

"To the past," Roland said. "To change something." He turned to look at Neeley. "We're given a Choice to go to a specific time and place in our past or join the Patrol. The time and place is, well, probably the most important moment of our life. Our past. We can go back and change it."

He fell silent and Neeley processed that. "How does Dane know that specific time and place?"

Roland's big shoulders shrugged. "They just know. Sin Fen, I guess, since she's the one who gave us the Choice when we were first recruited to the Patrol. You met her. She's got the Sight. She sees things. So I guess she can see the past and our lives. Or maybe they just got a really good dossier on us and know."

"What was—" Neeley began but she stopped. "Can you tell me what Nada's Choice was?"

"Yeah. Because it also was something you and I were involved with. In a way."

"How?"

"Nada was the best team sergeant I ever had," Roland said. "But I heard stories about his past. When he was in the regular Army and then Delta. He drank. He wasn't good with his wife and daughter and they left him. He had nothing left but the team and his wife ended up getting killed by an abusive man she married and his kid wasn't doing well. When we were given the Choice to join the Time Patrol, Nada's was whether he wanted to move forward with the team, or go back. To Afghanistan. 2005."

"Red Wings," Neeley said. Everyone in Special Ops knew about the most significant mission in that year in that country.

Roland nodded. "He went back. He made sure a guy was on one of the rescue choppers who hadn't originally been on it. So they both died in 2005. That changed things for Nada's kid for the better. But the guy who died with him, a Navy SEAL, well." Roland was trying to figure out something he hadn't really thought about. "Remember the guy we took out who was abusing his wife?"

Neeley nodded. "Yeah. The SEAL." She was much faster than Roland. "But if Nada got him on that chopper in '95 then . . . " She nodded. "That's why the body disappeared from the body bag."

"Yeah. It wasn't just about him abusing his wife and going after her again. That guy was working for some bad people. A rogue Russian Time Patrol team. You were involved in that too. The Ratnik."

"Okay, hold on," Neeley put her hands on Roland's broad shoulders, a physical anchor. "I see now. Why the Time Patrol is different."

"I guess it was a loop," Roland said. "We get them sometimes. I don't understand them. I don't think anyone does. I just don't think about it much."

"Okay," Neeley said. "This isn't like the Cellar. Where someone crosses a line and I sanction them. This is very different."

"It is."

Neeley still had her hands on his shoulders. She started him straight in the eyes. "What do you think I should do, Roland? Should I join the Team?"

"I'd like you on the Team," Roland said. He qualified. "I think I would. But I'd be worried. But I'm worried all the time anyway with what you do for the Cellar. But it's your decision."

"I know it's my decision. But I care about what you think. And you're on the team. I value your advice."

Roland flushed. He looked back out to sea. "Before the last mission, I'd have told you that having you on the team, well, we go on our missions alone. So even though we'd be teammates, that doesn't mean I can look out for you. Not that you need looking out for," he quickly added. "But we all ended up together on Valentines Day. And Doc—" He stopped.

Neeley slid her arms around him and embraced.

They stayed like that a long time, the only sound the waves breaking on the beach.

The Metropolitan Museum of Art
New York City

It was a pain in the ass to work under these conditions, but Ivar kind of, sort of, understand the concerns about the Internet not being secure from the Shadow. Any connection to the World Wide Web was a two way street, no matter how stringent the protocols.

So he kept rolling the chair back and forth between the two computers. One was linked to the web but guarded with the most secure software the NSA could provide, the other not connected. He used the former to gather information; the latter to summarize the information and run calculations.

The calculations were pretty pathetic so far.

The walls of the room were lined with whiteboard. The whiteboards were covered with Ivar's scrawl, mostly mathematical formulas.

Lots of formulas.

No solutions.

The room was buried deep underneath the Metropolitan Museum of Art, in the center of Manhattan on 5th Avenue, on the edge of Central Park. The building the public knew was an amalgamation of expansion from its founding almost 150 years ago. It now had over two million square feet of floor space.

The art inside the Met covered all of recorded history, over five thousand years. Essentially the lifespan of human civilization, which in the cosmic entirety is little more than the blink of any eye; unless it's your eye.

Ivar was six hundred feet below all this, nestled in the bedrock base of Manhattan Island. It, and the nearby HUB, could supposedly survive a direct nuclear blast on the museum above.

As if that mattered. Ivar had always found the military's pre-occupation with surviving an initial nuclear blast shortsighted, as if there wouldn't be far worse things down the line if that initiating event unfolded.

Plus there was the issue of would you be able to get out? And would you even want to get out into the world after such an event?

The computers were good. Top of the line. The one to the web didn't just go to the normal web. It also accessed the dark web, both the government's and the not-government's.

They were both pretty dark.

Ivar turned as the door creaked open on old iron hinges that needed some oil. Edith Frobish held her leather satchel to her chest as if it contained priceless documents.

Given her job, it might.

Then again, that's the way she always held it. Ivar couldn't imagine her and Eagle 'doing it'. He imagined whatever their 'it' was, involved a lot of intellectual conversation and literary allusions.

"I'm so sorry about Doc," Edith said as she entered and shut the door behind her. "I know the two of you were close."

That made Ivar pause. Had he been close to Doc? He hadn't even known the man's real name until Moms' ceremony. Of course, he didn't know Moms' or Roland's or Eagle's or Scout's real names either. Lara? No one knew who she was or where she came from. Ivar still wondered if he were the real Ivar after being duplicated in North Carolina, despite the affirmation of a Fate that he was.

Edith sat down next to him, putting her satchel on the desk. She was an art historian. Since art is an accurate recorder of a timeline, if the art changed, someone is trying to change the timeline. She was also the Time Patrol's archivist. With a dancer's tall body which she thought little of, and a prominent nose she also didn't concern herself with, she was all work. Except for—

"Where's Eagle?" Ivar asked, for lack of a reply to her concern.

"He had something he was ordered to do," Edith said.

"Of course," Ivar said.

Edith looked around at the whiteboards. "Catastrophe theory?"

"It's something Doc mentioned," Ivar said. "The number seven. The—"

"Do you have the letter?" Edith interrupted.

"What?"

"The letter," Edith said. "From Meyer Lansky. To Al Capone. Your letter of reference. It didn't come up in the debrief. Too much else happened."

Ivar nodded. He reached into his pocket and pulled it out. "I didn't think it was important. Like you said; a lot went on. Kind of got lost in all that."

"I'm not here to castigate you," Edith said. "Just tying up loose ends."

"That's your job, isn't it?" Ivar handed the letter to her. "Tying up loose ends?"

"No," Edith said. "My primary job is the art." She unfolded the letter and looked at it for several seconds. Then she put it on the desk and turned it around so he could see. Not that she needed to turn it around. It was blank.

Ivar stared at it. "The loop must have closed when Strings died. He couldn't have gotten Lansky to write it if he wasn't alive." He thought about it for a second. "But then wouldn't the letter itself be gone, not just the words?"

"I don't know," Edith said. She indicated the mathematical formulas on the whiteboard. "Where does that fit in all of this?"

"I haven't gotten very far with it," Ivar admitted.

"I don't think you'll get very far with it," Edith said.

"How do you know that?"

"Ever wonder why art is an indicator of history, of a timeline, and math isn't?"

"Math changes," Ivar said.

"Exactly. Art evolves, but art from a thousand years ago remains fixed. Math from a thousand years ago might no longer be valid as new theories, new calculations come along. Much the same as physics. A theorem that was held to be sacrosanct fifty years is debunked. A new one takes its place. And there's another reason."

"And that is?"

"Because catastrophe theory is wrong," Edith said.

"How do you know?"

"Other timelines have done the hard work. And ended up nowhere because it simply is a ruse. Some of them paid dearly for doing that work."

"'A ruse'?"

"We've looked into it since you brought it up," Edith said. "We believe catastrophe theory is a honey-trap."

"A what?"

"You must have dozed through that part of your training at Bragg." Edith said it with a smile to remove any criticism. "The Soviet Union would use sex in what's called a honey trap. Women, men, whatever a target's proclivity was. To lure them in." She indicated the boards. "For scientists, it tends to be numbers. Theorems. Checking data. The Shadow knows this."

Ivar understood. "A honey trap is planted. It's deliberate."

"Exactly," Edith said. "And we think catastrophe theory is a plant. We believe the Shadow introduced it in the fifties via an agent or a Valkyrie or by whatever means. It percolated until a brilliant mathematician jumped on it and promulgated it. The Shadow knows that eventually those trying to figure out the rule of seven will delve into it. Thus . . ."

"All right," Ivar said. "Let's say that's true. Then what am I supposed to do?"

"We're not saying stop," Edith said. "We saying perhaps look at it a different way. If catastrophe theory was planted by the Shadow, what are they trying to keep us from seeing?"

"That's a good point," Ivar said. "When people want you too look one way, sometimes it's because they don't want you looking somewhere else."

"Come with me," Edith said.

Ivar followed and they left the room. They walked down a brick-layered corridor of indeterminate age. They passed a pair of heavily armed security guards who didn't say a word.

They got on the elevator to the Museum proper and made the six hundred foot ride in silence. It was after closing, the large halls empty of the throngs of tourists.

Edith negotiated back hallways. She pushed open a door into a gallery. Walked up to a painting. "There. Monet. *The Water Lily Pond.*"

Ivar didn't say anything. She led him to another exhibit. "*The Death of Socrates* by Jacques-Louis David. It depicts what happened after Socrates was accused of denying the Gods and corrupting the young. He was given a choice. Renounce his beliefs or drink a cup of hemlock."

"He's reaching for the cup," Ivar said.

"Indeed."

"Do you have a point?"

"You're going to have to approach things differently," Edith said.

"In what way?"

Edith touched Ivar's chest. "You're going to have to use your heart as well as your brain. Do you feel Socrates' bravery and the anguish of those around him looking at that?" She indicated the painting.

Ivar gave a small nod. "He's not willing to compromise."

"Why?" Edith asked.

"I've got a PhD in physics, not philosophy."

"You can think for yourself. That's all philosophy is."

"If he renounced what he believed in," Ivar said, "then it wipes out everything. Not just his living, but everything he lived for."

"Exactly," Edith said. "All that in a painting. But to have to explain it to someone? How would you program that into a computer?"

"It could be done," Ivar said.

"Really?"

"Maybe. If AI advances far enough."

"Do you want AI to advance to that point?"

"You're trying to make a point," Ivar said. "Why not just tell me?"

"Because people rarely get a point told to them," Edith said. "They have to feel it prick their skin. Worm its way in. Make them feel. And eventually it blossoms into something they believe they came up with themselves. Come on." Edith took his arm, pulling him along. "We got this painting on loan from MOMA."

"'MOMA'?"

"Metropolitan Museum of Art."

"It's a cartoon," Ivar said.

"It's a painting based on a cartoon panel," Edith said. "It's called, easily enough as you can see, *Drowning Girl*." The face of a woman in swirling water, one hand out of the water, but not raised for succor, but rather protest. A dialogue box above her read:

I DON'T CARE! I'D RATHER SINK THAN CALL BRAD FOR HELP!

"Since when do cartoon drawings make it into museums?" Ivar asked.

Edith didn't say anything, letting Ivar stare at it.

"She must really hate this Brad guy to die before she'd ask him for help," he finally said.

"Would a machine do that?"

"No."

"Is the Shadow a machine?"

"We don't know," Ivar said. "We assume it's another timeline. A human timeline as we've only run into alternate Earths."

"We don't use computers at the Possibility Palace," Edith said, "because we know the Shadow can use them to attack us. If the Shadow thinks computers are so vulnerable, do you think it, or let's say, they, would rely on them?"

"Doubtful," Ivar said.

"So why do we think a computer can solve a human problem?"

Area 51, Nevada

"Lose-lose," Colonel Orlando said. "Supposed to be the best measure of a man."

"The Kobyashi Maru scenario," Eagle said.

"What I said."

They were at a remote, concrete airfield on the Area 51 military reservation. The landing strip had no designation and lacked buildings or hangers. It was one of several outlying field that dotted the 4,531 square miles of the Nevada Test and Training Range. Most were abandoned and half buried in sand. Technically abandoned that is. In the covert world nothing is ever abandoned.

Not even people. Orlando was old, tired and drunk. The first was a product of nature, the second from the job, the third also from the job; so he said. When the drinking had gotten to be too much, he'd been kindly exited from the Nightstalkers and shifted into Support. Many would have viewed it as a demotion. Orlando had accepted it as an inevitability and preferable to a Sanction.

"How is everyone?" Orlando asked. A distant speck appeared in the sky, a plane heading in this direction. "Moms?"

"Okay."

"You say that with a hitch in your voice." Orlando might be ROAD—retired on active duty—but there was a reason he'd initially been recruited into the Nightstalkers many years ago. Even more significantly, he'd been good enough to survive long enough to be shuttled off to this job.

Very few made it that far. Most ended up with their names carved into a table.

"She took a forty-five slug to the thigh on our last mission."

"Ouch," Orlando said. "That hurts. Speaking from experience. Not my leg. Elbow." He rubbed the offending appendage. "From behind. Hit the elbow, bounced up along the bone and came out my shoulder. I was lucky. Full metal jacket. If it had been one of them cop killer 9mm bullets, it would have destroyed my elbow. Probably would have lost the arm. Like that shit head Frasier. Please tell me he got killed on a mission." He said it without much hope.

"He doesn't go on missions any more," Eagle said.

"Then tell me someone fragged his ass. Or he got Sanctioned?"

"No such luck. He was shifted to support."

"A pity." Orlando pulled a flask out of his camouflage fatigue jacket pocket and took a swig. He offered it to Eagle, etiquette more than expecting to be taken up, which it wasn't. "That new girl. Lara. What's with her?"

"She's been helpful," Eagle said.

"Uh-huh. And Scout? I like her too."

"Scout's fine."

"Am I going to have to go through the roster?" Orlando groused. "Ain't many left. Ivar came on later. You're standing here. You appear functional. Have all your pieces and parts. Roland?"

"He's got a girlfriend."

It took a lot to shock Orlando, but that qualified. "Bull."

"Seriously."

"What kind of woman would be crazy enough to hang with Roland?"

"She's an assassin. Works for the Cellar."

"Oh." Orlando nodded. "That makes sense. What about Doc? He was a Nightstalker. Thinks too much, but someone has to do it."

Eagle gave the briefest shake of his head. "We lost him on the last mission. He sacrificed himself so the rest of the team could make it out alive."

Orlando sighed deeply. Took another swig. Put the flask away. "Explains the urgency to recruit all of a sudden. Not that I haven't been looking." He nodded toward the plane, which was about three miles off, but still at five thousand feet altitude. Both Eagle and Orlando could recognize the make, both from silhouette and the sound of the engines: the venerable C-130 Hercules cargo plane. "Got a dozen fools on board. Pick of the litter. Well, most of them. Best of the best and all that crap."

"You tend not to take the pick of the litter," Eagle observed. "You pick the outcasts."

Orlando smiled. "Yeah. Hard to find the right mix. Someone who can think on their own, be a pain in the ass, but in the crunch work with the team. A dying trait." He got serious. "Sorry. No pun intended there. Did Moms retire Doc's name?"

"Yes. We have a new table. His name is on it."

"As long as we remember his name," Orlando murmured, "he lives on."

Eagle squinted. "The back ramp is down. The grenade scenario?"

"A version of it," Orlando said. "I've been thinking about lose-lose."

"Is that why you said '*supposed* to the best measure of a man'?" Eagle asked.

"Yeah. The Kobe Bryant Star Trek thingie you mentioned. Everyone acts like Kirk did the right thing by cheating. And we know cheating is important. If you ain't cheating, you ain't trying. One of the first lessons you learn in Special Ops. But it's more important to evaluate how someone reacts to an unexpected situation. Some times you got to follow rules. Kirk essentially changed the scenario, therefore the scenario was no longer valid. The issue is that he actually didn't take the real test."

"He did," Eagle said. "According to Star Trek backstory. Twice. Failed both times."

"Failed which way?"

"I don't remember," Eagle said.

"Would be nice to know. Makes a difference. Did he follow the rules or break the rules?"

People came off the back ramp as the C-130 passed overhead.

"I count eleven jumpers," Eagle said.

"Hmm," was Orlando's response. "What makes you think they have parachutes?"

"We're not supposed to kill them," Eagle said.

"I suppose." Orlando sounded disappointed.

A parachute blossomed open. Then another. And another. Until all eleven were floating down to earth.

The C-130 banked and lost altitude, lining up on the runway.

Eagle was tracking the jumpers. "They're going to land on the far side of the runway." He turned for the Jeep.

"Where you going?" Orlando asked.

"To get them."

"Can't fit all of them in there," Orlando said. "They got feet. They can walk."

"All right," Eagle said. "What exactly was the scenario in there?"

Orlando shrugged. "Doesn't matter."

"How can you evaluate them then?"

"Already did."

The C-130 touched down. Sand and dirt blew about as it slowed, then taxied toward Orlando and Eagle. It came to a halt facing away at an angle, the back ramp lowering to touch the concrete, engines still running. In the distance, the jumpers were gathering their parachutes, rolling them up. The familiar smell of turboprop exhaust bathed Eagle and Orlando with its essence, eliciting subliminal memories.

"Come on," Orlando said. He walked toward the plane. Eagle followed.

There was one person sitting on the red webbing along the outer edge in the large cargo bay. Orlando waved at him.

The man didn't respond. He was dressed in a dull gray jumpsuit. He sported long, disheveled gray hair to his shoulders, and a gray beard streaked with white. He appeared asleep, head lolled back.

Or dead.

Orlando had to shout to be heard above the sound of the engines. "End of the line."

"I'll not be going anywhere with the likes of you, Orlando," the man said with a Scottish accent. "Nothing good can come of that."

"Nothing good came of the last thing you did," Orlando said, "considering I got you out of the Penitentiary."

"A temporary setback." The old man opened his eyes and looked at Eagle, then back at Orlando. "I recognized your little game. All the little ducklings jumped. One was kind enough to offer to do a tandem with me, seeing as there weren't enough chutes. I kindly thanked the lad, but told him I preferred where I was. Appears I was correct as to the status of the pilots and the plane. What a surprise the plane didn't crash. I was quite terrified."

"Eagle, meet Angus. Angus, this is Eagle."

"I presume that was not the name passed to you by your parents," Angus said. He stood and offered his hand. "And it's Angus. Never Gus."

Eagle took it and was surprised at the firm grip. Angus was solidly built, the same height as Eagle at six foot, but broader, with a barrel chest. He was old, but he was in shape. How old was hard to tell. His face was weathered, leathery, deep lines etched around the eyes. Anywhere from a hard fifty-something to an excellent seventy-something.

"Let's go," Orlando said, indicating the ramp and the waiting Jeep.

"Do I have a choice?" Angus asked.

Orlando shrugged. "The plane can take you back to the Big House. Or you can get off and come with us."

"It's peaceful back there," Angus said, as if he were seriously debating the decision.

"I'm sure it is," Orlando said. "No demands on you. I'm sure the other fellows leave you alone, being as you're such a manly man and all that."

Angus grinned, revealing terrible teeth. Revealing there wasn't much of a dental plan in the Big House.

"That I am, that I am. I'm getting quite a bit of reading done. Catching up on all those years I didna have the time. Books a smart person is supposed to read in their lifetime. I suppose you've already made it through the list, but I'm a bit slow."

"I'd appreciate it if you came," Orlando said. "Eagle is the reader. You two can chat."

"And why would you appreciate it?" Angus asked.

"You would add a voice of experience and reason to our organization," Orlando said.

Angus laughed. "Now you're pulling my leg. And what organization will that be?"

"Can't tell you unless you come," Orlando said.

"If it's got the likes of you in it, that's not exactly sending the recruiting poster child out, is it now?" Angus asked.

Orlando shrugged. "Maybe it is if we want the likes of you."

"Ah well," Angus said. "I'm sure this promises to be some sort of grand adventure." He held out his hand and Orlando produced the flask. Angus took a deep draught. "Still drinking swill. We'll have to work on that." He took another drink of the swill. "Let's be off then." He put the flask in his pocket and walked off the ramp.

Possibility Palace

The pneumatic tube behind Dane delivered a scroll with a resounding thump.

A special sound, because the paper was a unique weight, extra thick, and rarely used.

Dane opened the tube and retrieved the scroll. He placed it on his table and used some of the thick personnel files to hold it open.

It was his equivalent of a Zevon; an alert of a pending attack by the Shadow. It listed the day of the year and the six years of the coming bubbles in time along with locations. Dane scanned it:

31 OCTOBER
1517—WITTENBERG CASTLE CHURCH, GERMANY
1692—SALEM, MASSACHUSETTS
1828—ZULULAND, SOUTH AFRICA
1941—NORTH SEA, COORDINATES: 51.983°N 27.083°W
USS REUBEN JAMES
1984: PRIME MINISTER'S RESIDENCE, NEW DELHI,
INDIA
ZERO DAY—ZERO YEAR. 60 HUDSON STREET, NEW
YORK, NY

He stared at the last line, trying to process it.

The door to his office opened without a knock. There was only one person who would do that.

"I saw it," Sin Fen said.

"I don't understand," Dane said. "What is Zero Day-Zero Year? When is it?"

"I don't know the entire thing," Sin Fen said. "But I do know what a Zero Day is. It's a computer term, which makes sense, since that address is a building that houses one of the world's major Internet hubs. A Zero Day is two connected things: an unpatched software hole that the creator isn't aware of; and the code a hacker will use to exploit that hole. Zero Day is the very first day that software is being used and the hole is there."

Dane realized something. "Remember Y-Two-K? When we thought computer programs would crash because they could only used two digits for the year and when they went from nine-nine to zero-zero?"

Sin Fen nodded.

"What if a Zero Day leads to a Zero Year?" Dane asked. "Everything rebooting or starting over? That means this Zero Year could be any year in the past, but it has to be relatively recent, after the invention of the Internet. It might even be the year 1999. 31 October would be two months before then. Maybe something that sets up a deep problem on Y2K?"

"Perhaps," Sin Fen allowed. "Regardless, the bubble will open in whatever year it is." Something occurred to her. "What is Ivar doing?"

"Working on the Turing Time Computer in the Met secure room.."

"He has to shut down now!" Sin Fen said.

"You mean he's getting hacked right now?" Dane asked.

"No. But a hack is coming, or rather it came, unless it's stopped." Sin Fen said. "And if the Shadow is behind it and it's a Zero Day, we can be sure it's going to be a bad one."

The Metropolitan Museum of Art
New York City

The door was shoved open and one of the guards came in, fast and hard, as they trained in the Kill House at Fort Bragg. Ivar was still turning in the chair when the man fired on full automatic.

His bullets hit the computer linked to the Internet, blasting pieces of metal and screen.

A piece of screen hit Ivar in the check, drawing some blood. Ivar belatedly dove for cover as the guard swung his weapon toward the other computer and emptied the rest of his magazine. The guard automatically pulled out another magazine and slammed it home.

"Sorry, sir," he said to Ivar, sounding not sorry at all. In fact, he seemed rather pleased to be able to shoot something. "Orders."

And then he left the room, the smell of gunpowder heavy in the air, the floor and desks littered with the remains of the computers. Ivar reached up and felt his cheek. A scratch.

At that moment Ivar's Satphone alerted: *Lawyers, Guns and Money.*

An Island Off The Coast Of Puerto Rico

Neeley was the first to break the embrace. "I have to call Hannah."

"Okay," Roland said.

Neeley smiled and kissed him. "You are one of a kind, Roland."

He blushed. "Really? Is that good?"

"I think you're the only person who wouldn't have asked me what I was going to tell her."

"It's your decision," Roland said, not understanding why it was so special that he hadn't asked.

"It is. Thank you."

Neeley pulled out her Satphone. Roland started to move away, but she reached out and took his forearm as the phone was answered on the first ring.

"Yes, Neeley?"

"I'm going," Neeley said.

"I will miss you," Hannah said. "We've walked a long road together from St. Louis."

"We have," Neeley agreed.

"I'm glad you have Roland," Hannah said. "He's a good man."

"He is."

"If you ever need anything, well . . ." Hannah's voice trailed off.

"I know."

"I really don't know what to say," Hannah said. "I've never said good-bye to someone like this. Someone who I owe my life to. And more."

"Until we meet again is good enough," Neeley said.

"Until we meet again." The phone went dead.

Neeley turned to Roland.

"I'm sorry," Roland said.

"For what?"

"That you no longer work for your friend."

Neeley smiled. "When you put it that way, perhaps I made the right decision."

"I think—" Roland began, but then his Satphone chimed: *Lawyers, Guns and Money.*

He pulled it out and looked at the screen.

IS NEELEY WITH US? IF SO, WE NEED HER. IF NOT, NEED TO KNOW ASAP

He simply showed it to her.

They turned as a low-flying helicopter came swooping in.

Airspace, United States

"Right fancy bird this is," Angus said as he settled into the co-pilot's seat of the Snake. "Orlando is sleeping one off. Or two or three. Mainly sleeping off his previous life."

The Snake, a jet engine, tilt-wing prototype, that wasn't even supposed to be built yet, was on autopilot, heading east over the US.

"He's a good man," Eagle said, a bit defensively.

Angus laughed. "Oh, laddie, you don't have to tell me that. Do you know *why* he tips the bottle so much?"

"Not the particulars," Eagle said.

"The devil is in the details," Angus said. "He's a better man than many a man."

"How do you two know each other?"

"The devil knows those details," Angus said. "This buggy of yours. Pretty fancy. No markings or tail number. Last I read, no one had a jet tilt wing operational. But we get the papers and magazines behind the times in the Big House."

"Are you talking Leavenworth?" Eagle asked, referring to that Federal Penitentiary.

"No, they were going to send me there, but decided it wasn't appropriate for a man of my, well, shall we say, resume."

"ADX Florence?" Eagle asked.

"You are a knowledgeable man," Angus noted. "Most call it simply Supermax, albeit there was nothing particularly super about it. The food is horrendous, I can tell you."

"And what kind of resume requires the Supermax?" Eagle asked. "Prisoners are sent there either because they're so dangerous, they're so notorious, they're an extreme escape risk, or they're predicated to attacking guards in a violent manner."

"You do know a lot," Angus said. "I'd say I qualify on a few of those tick marks, although I wouldn't harm a guard. Just doing their job, although some enjoy it a tad too much. However, there's no upside to taking on one of those fellows, not when they have the key." Angus sighed. "But enough about me." He indicated Eagle. "You have no uniform. We were out in the desert, best I could tell, sitting in the back as I was, somewhere in Nevada. We have Orlando recruiting me and I'm not even a citizen of this fair country of yours. So perhaps you give me a wee bit of idea what I've signed on to?"

"The devil would be in those details," Eagle said, "and I'm not the devil to tell them to you. My boss will do that."

"Is he a devil?"

"No, but he's a driven man."

"Ah, those can be the worst of men or the best of men, depends on what direction they be driving."

"He's good man."

"Hesitation in that," Angus said. "You have doubts. That concerns me as it seems I'm part of this gig. What do you know about me?"

"Not a thing," Eagle admitted. "Orlando didn't tell me a word. But you both made it clear you were in prison and your choice was come on this gig, as you call it, or go back. To the Supermax in Colorado."

"That is so," Angus said. "And I be figuring you want to know why?"

"Up to if you want to disclose," Eagle said.

"Don't be coy, lad. That would be a natural curiosity. At least in the outside world. But it is a question that is never asked on the inside."

"So why?" Eagle asked.

"I killed a man."

"Self-defense?"

"Oh, no. Deliberate offense."

Eagle waited, but there was nothing else. Until his phone went off, playing the familiar tune: *Lawyers, Guns and Money*

Angus was pleased. "Warren Zevon. I fancy his tune *Roland the Headless Thompson Gunner.*"

"We have a Roland on the team," Eagle said, checking the phone. "Named for that Roland."

"A Roland and an Eagle," Angus said. "So you boys make up names for yourselves? Sort of like playing school or something?"

"It's a ritual. We leave our old lives behind when we join the team."

"Rituals can be useful," Angus said. "But can one truly leave their old life behind?" He didn't wait for an answer. "Ever been to the pub in Spain run by the fellow Warren wrote it with? Ex-merc. Davey. Serves good scotch, not the swill Orlando carries. I passed through once when Warren was in residence. '75 I believe it was. Ah, those were the days. Manly men and all that. And the sheep, right scared they were."

Possibility Palace

Only someone with extreme focus of duty would have been able to pick up the ring tone through the medicated semi-conscious state.

Moms was such a person. She fought against the chemical lethargy, struggling into consciousness.

The phone went silent and she slumped back on the bed. She looked at the IV in her arm, then at the drip.

"Frak it," she muttered.

With her other hand she slid the needle out of her arm. She slithered out of the bed, not quite able to stand, and crawled across to the closet that held her clothing and gear. She fumbled through her old, worn, combat vest until she found a small metal vial. It took her a while to unscrew the lid. Then, with a shaking hand, she poured the pills inside on the floor. She peered down, knowing she had to make sure she took the right one, or else she'd be comatose, if not worse.

Reasonably confident she's sorted it out and had the correct one from the small stash Doc had issued to each team member a long time ago, Moms put it in her mouth.

*****

35

"Frak me," Scout muttered as her phone Zevoned, the sound echoed by Lara's.

They were sitting cross-legged in a room next to the Team Room. This was nominally the 'rec room' although it was dominated by Roland's weights. A piece of log was in one corner, set on end, with a dozen knives, hatchets, and other sharp instruments stuck in it.

Scout and Lara had been watching the five years out of date flat screen TV. It only played DVDs—no cable in time travel.

"We're here already for frak's sake." Scout silenced the ring.

Lara did the same.

"We've got some time," Scout said. "The bubbles don't open right way. And the team is assembling. We can finish this episode. I just cannot believe you've never seen Buffy. I mean, seriously. They had Buffy in Wichita, right?"

"It's strange," Lara said. "When I focus, I can't remember seeing *any* television. But I know I had to have. I know what television is. It's very weird. Like my brain is split. And I'm not sure I'm from Wichita. I kind of don't know where I'm from."

"Join the club," Scout said. She hit the play button.

*****

Dane was silent as Edith Frobish and Frasier entered his office. He indicated for them to sit down on the other side of his desk. He had a thick scroll open in front of him, but he wasn't looking at it. Instead he had a distant gaze, as if looking through the wall to the Pit.

He finally spoke. "31 October."

"Halloween?" Edith said, her mind racing through history. "Luther nailed his ninety-five theses to the cathedral door in Wittenberg on the 31st of October, in 1517. That has to be one of the years."

"It is," Dane confirmed. "But . . ."

The other two waited, disturbed by an uncertain Dane. "One of them isn't specified," he finally said. "It just says 'Zero Day, Zero Year.' There is a location. 60 Hudson Street, New York City."

Dane slid a single piece of paper to each of them. He waited while they scanned the years and locations.

"Zero Day?" Frasier said. "That's a computer thing, isn't it?"

"It is," Dane said. "Sin Fen is digging into it."

"Oh!" Edith exclaimed as she read, immediately embarrassed.

"Salem?" Dane asked.

Edith nodded. "A terrible, terrible time. Who are you sending?"

"That's what we have to decide. For all the missions."

"Did you get a reply from Neeley?" Frasier asked.

"She said yes," Dane said. "She's with Roland. I alerted both."

"She's not up to speed on operations here," Edith said.

"Unless Roland has talked to her," Frasier said. "Pillow talk."

Dane shook his head. "I'm not even sure Roland, or Neeley for that matter, has a pillow. And Roland doesn't break rules." He indicated the paper. "A wide array of assignments. Suggestions?"

"Eagle obviously gets 1828," Frasier said.

"That early," Edith said, being a bit more circumspect about it, "there were very few whites in South Africa. Cape Town had been established, but there were only a handful of trading posts along the coast. Most maps labeled the interior of sub-Saharan Africa simply as unknown."

"All right," Dane said. "Eagle. 1828. Since Neeley is new, we give her the most straightforward and in line with her skills and experiences. 1984. India. It's also the closest to our time. She's done her share of assassinations; it should be easier for her to make sure one happens."

The other two agreed.

Dane looked at the paper. "That leaves us with Ivar, Scout, Lara and Roland. And it's obvious Roland has to be on the *Reuben James*. A young woman would be too obvious. A destroyer in the North Atlantic doesn't fit Ivar. Roland is 1941." He penciled that in. "So which one gets Wittenberg?"

"We still don't know who Lara is," Frasier pointed out. "And technically, she hasn't been on a mission."

"They're both so young," Dane said, more to himself. "Scout has shown herself to be resilient. And she has the Sight. We don't know what the hell Lara has."

"We don't even know who she is," Frasier repeated.

"And you have nothing further?" Dane asked.

Frasier shook his head.

"Scout's come through for us twice," Edith said, trying to keep them on task.

"I notice you seem to be ignoring Ivar as a possibility for Wittenberg," Frasier said.

"I'm not ignoring him," Edith said. "His skill set points to Zero Day."

Dane nodded. "Ivar gets Zero Day. He was actually on the computer in the secure room at the Met when I Zevoned him." Dane leaned back in the chair. "Salem is weird. So let's send weird. Lara gets that. Which leaves Scout with Wittenberg."

"Has Hannah okayed bringing Neeley on board?" Edith asked.

"I discussed the possibility with Hannah," Dane said. "She left it up to Neeley."

"But she hasn't made the Choice," Edith said. "The real Choice one about joining the team."

"Mission takes priority," Dane said. "But Sin Fen is here. She can meet with Neeley and give her the Choice prior to deployment."

"What if she decides to go back?" Frasier asked. "What about 1984 and New Delhi?"

"Then I'll have to make one of you operational," Dane said. "So you'd better hope she doesn't choose to go back."

The Mission Briefing

The Possibility Palace, Headquarters, Time Patrol
Where? Can't tell you. When? Can't tell you

SCOUT WAS THE FIRST to enter the team room. She was dressed in a black bodice and skirt, with flat leather shoes. She was already pulling at the bodice, trying to relieve the pressure. Her short dyed-red hair was covered with a black French hood.

She had a pair of spectacles in her hand. She placed them on the table in the center of the team room, next to Doc's name. Looking over at one wall, she noted the black-green scale Roland had taken from Grendel and the original Order of Merit ribbon, the forerunner of the Purple Heart, which Eagle had received directly from George Washington.

Now they had another relic of the past: Benjamin Franklin's spectacles, a gift to Doc from the old man for saving his life during the 1776 Staten Island Peace Talks.

The door opened and Eagle came in.

"Whoa!" Scout said. "You look ready for war."

"And almost naked," Eagle added. He wore the garb of a Zulu warrior, which consisted mainly of weapons along with the scant garment of an apron, front and rear. He indicated the arm and legs bands. "The *amashoba*. Made from cow tails. They're designed to make the wearer appear bulkier and more powerful."

"Cool," Scout said. "It works."

"I'd prefer body armor." He put the five-foot high shield on the table, along with the two weapons.

Scout pointed at them. "You can explain the spear and club and shield when Roland gets here. I don't want you to have to do it again."

Eagle smiled. "Early nineteenth century for me. Some time after Shaka united the Zulu kingdom."

"Unless you're going as a re-enactor," Scout said. "You know, like those guys who dress up in Civil War stuff. I think there are re-enactors for every soldier who ever existed. I'm sure there are Zulu re-enactors."

"I doubt I'm going to a tourist event." Eagle indicated the spear. "The blade is Naga metal." He noted Scout's outfit. "Middle ages. Not poor, but not rich either."

"But no hot showers, right?" Scout said. "It's tight and the cloth is really irritating. Still, it's a step up from the robes I've been wearing before. I bet it still smells bad wherever and whenever I'm going."

"Most likely," Eagle said. "Let's hope—"

He was interrupted as the next member of the team joined them.

"A sailor, again," Roland said, disappointed. Mainly because he didn't have any weapons.

"More modern than your last," Eagle said. "World War II era."

Roland forgot his disappointment upon seeing Eagle's array of killing tools. "Can I?" He indicated the spear. Roland hefted it. "Kind of short isn't it?"

"It's an *iklwa*," Eagle said. "It's not made for throwing. The name comes from the sucking sound it makes when you pull it out of someone's body." It was short of being what most would consider a true spear, with a two-foot shaft and a large, eight-inch long, wide blade. "A warrior could be executed for losing one. Shaka Zulu, who invented it, also forbade his warriors from throwing it. It's designed for stabbing."

Roland was getting the feel. "Nice. Like a big bayonet."

"A bayonet with no rifle," Scout noted. "I'd rather have a rifle."

Roland ignored her. He handed the spear back. "And the club?"

"The *iwisa*," Eagle said. He passed it to Roland.

"Heavy," Roland said. "It would make a nice dent in someone's skull. The shield?"

Eagle gave that to him. It was five feet tall and made of cowhide.

"The *isihlangu*," Eagle said. "It replaced a smaller shield. The theory is, that besides being protection, you use the edge of the *isihlangu* to pull the enemy's shield toward you, thus exposing him to a thrust from the *iklwa*. Shaka completely revamped the way Zulus fought in terms of weapons and tactics. This means I'm going at the time of Shaka or just after. Because later on, the Zulus started using longer spears, more suited to throwing. And—"

But he stopped when the door opened and Neeley entered.

"Welcome," Eagle said. He glanced at Roland, then back at her. "When were you recruited?"

"Not long ago," Neeley said. "Actually, I was asked if I wanted to join the team, and then right after I told Hannah I would, Roland got alerted. And I was ordered to come with him."

"We're short one," Eagle said, "since Moms is non-operational. I assume Dane made a command decision."

Neeley was dressed in khaki pants and shirt, with leather, half-calf boots. "Any clue what this outfit means?"

"Relatively modern," Eagle said. "But it's rather generic."

She looked at Roland. "A sailor?"

He nodded. "Eagle says World War Two."

"Okay," Neeley said, for lack of anything else. She looked at Scout and Eagle. "Definitely different than what I'm used to. How do we find out when and where we're going?"

"Dane will be in to brief us," Eagle said. "Once everyone is here. We still need Lara and Ivar."

"Don't count on finding out too much from Dane," Scout warned Neeley. "Vague doesn't begin to describe these mission briefings."

"We get enough," Roland said. "Don't worry," he added to Neeley. "It will be all right."

Lara entered, looking none too thrilled in her later Middle Ages outfit. "Feel like I'm in a Shakes-dude play."

"You're a bit later than Shakespeare," Eagle said.

"When were the Dark Ages?" Lara asked.

"That's more likely for Scout," Eagle said as he checked out Lara's clothing.

"Gee, thanks," Scout said.

41

"You're more seventeenth century," Eagle said to Lara.

"No hot showers," Scout told her.

"We're only gone for twenty-four hours max," Roland said. "I've gone three months without a shower."

"I bet that was thrilling for those around you," Scout said.

Ivar entered, upset, a small line of blood on one cheek. He was dressed in his normal old jeans and gray t-shirt.

"What happened to you?" Eagle asked.

"The security man at the Met shot my computers," Ivar said. "Then I got Zevoned."

"Why'd he shoot the computers?" Eagle asked.

"I got no idea," Ivar said. "He just shot them to pieces, said he was sorry, and left."

"Were you looking at porn again?" Scout asked.

Ivar gave her a dirty look. "And they told me I didn't need to change. I don't get it." He looked around. "We know Moms can't go. What—"

The door opened and Edith pushed Moms' wheelchair in. Moms had Edith's satchel on her lap. Dane followed, trundling a small cart and shutting the door behind.

"What happened to you?" Moms asked Ivar.

He repeated his brief story as Dane went to the board.

"There's a reason for that," Dane said as Ivar finished. "I'm sorry such drastic measures had to be taken, but we couldn't take a chance."

"A chance on what?" Ivar asked. "The guy didn't even say hi. He just started blasting away. I thought he was after me for a moment."

"If he was after you," Dane said, "you wouldn't know it was coming."

"Great," Ivar said.

Dane waved off the comment. "Sorry. We had to shut down any computer link, even the most secure one."

"Why?" Moms asked.

"One of the missions," Dane said. "I don't know the extent yet, but Sin Fen will be in here shortly to explain. Can you bear with me for a bit?"

Ivar nodded.

Dane went right to business, picking up a piece of chalk and writing a year on it.

1517

Before he could speak, Eagle was ahead of him, the most important event of that year readily available from his prodigious memory. "31 October, right?"

Dane nodded. "Hallows Eve."

"You mean Halloween," Scout said.

"Yes," Dane said. "And please, no jokes about trick or treating. Edith, tell them about the historical significance of the day."

"The Feast of All Saints is on the first of November," Edith said. "But the celebration begins the previous evening. The holiday precedes Christianity, as many do. The Celtic festival of Samhain marked the end of the harvest season and the beginning of winter. It started on the evening of 31 October and ran through sunset on the 1st. The Celts actually viewed a day to be from sundown to sundown, rather than the way we view a day in the opposite manner. The Catholic Church uses the celebration as a way to commemorate those who have gone to heaven."

"Count us out," Scout said.

"Thus," Edith plowed on, "the date is noted for a connection with the dead. The tradition of putting on a costume and trick and treating is a relatively recent thing."

"Commercialization," Eagle said. "It's the second largest retail—" he stopped himself.

"Thanks," Dane said, when Eagle didn't give facts and figures on Halloween. "What matters is where and when each of you is going." He pointed the chalk at Eagle. "As your team sergeant brought up, the most significant event of the year 1517 was Martin Luther posting his Ninety-five Theses on the 31st of October on the Wittenberg Castle Church door. And that's your mission, Scout."

"Ninety-five Theses of what?" Scout asked.

Edith fielded the question. "It was the beginning of Protestantism. Luther challenged the Roman Catholic Church on some of its principles, primarily the practice of indulgences, which was paying priests and the church to buy one's way into heaven."

"Doubt that worked," Scout said.

"It was nice for those who got the money," Eagle said. "Primarily the church."

"Others had challenged the Catholic Church before," Edith said, "but Luther came at a unique time. Many were discontent with the Church and, most importantly, it occurred as the printing press was available. Thus Luther's theses could be widely disseminated. Because of Luther, the Church splintered between the Roman Catholics and the Protestants. The repercussions of that—" she shook her head, a bit overwhelmed with the possibilities.

"Okay," Scout said. "So I have to make sure this thing gets posted?"

"If that's what the Shadow is trying to block," Dane said. "It could be going after Luther directly. Perhaps an assassination attempt. While it's likely someone else would have eventually challenged the Church, Luther was the key. There's no doubt his failure to do so would be a Cascade event and change our timeline."

"Got it," Scout said. "But if they're sending someone to kill him, it will most likely be a Legion. Gonna give me something more than this skirt to fight with?"

"We've accepted that armament is essential," Dane said. He went to the cart and opened it. He lifted out a stack of identical wooden boxes and put them on the table. He slid one over to Scout.

She flipped up the lid. "Cool." She pulled out a dagger.

Dane gave each member of the team a similar box, except Ivar. "We told you before Nine-Eleven that we were going to make one for every team member." He looked at Ivar. "You still have yours, correct?"

Ivar drew his from a sheath in the back of his pants.

"They're made of Naga steel," Dane said. "You can puncture a Valkyrie's armor with that. Pretty much cut through anything with enough force."

"Not a Grendel's scales," Roland said. "You have to go for the armpit, the base of the skull, or into the mouth."

Scout slid the blade into the accompanying sheath. "Thanks. I feel a bit better. But isn't it possible the Shadow maybe just wants Luther to have maybe 90 Theses? Or add five more and have 100? Change some of them?"

"Of course it's possible," Dane said. "You'll have a copy of the Theses in your download."

"I'm going to have to read them all?" Scout was aghast.

"Please, let's not get into it," Dane said. "We know there are an infinite number of possibilities. Your last mission indicated the need to be prepared for just about anything. That's why you people were chosen to be on the team. You're the best—"

"I was in the wrong place at the wrong time," Ivar interrupted.

"Me too," Scout said.

"Ditto," Lara said.

"You've gone on missions and you're still alive," Dane said.

"Doc isn't," Scout countered. "Mac isn't."

Neeley spoke up. "I think I'm supposed to make some sort of Choice even though I volunteered?"

Dane was grateful for the interruption. "You'll go with Sin Fen after this briefing and make your choice. For the rest of you, you're the Time Patrol. You've all been on missions. You've all traveled in time. You've defeated Grendels and Valkyries and Pandora and most importantly, you've beaten the Shadow every single time. The clock is ticking. Can we move on?"

Silence meant assent, so Dane wrote on the board:

1984

"Neeley. You're going to New Delhi. Gandhi's assassination."

Neeley frowned. "Mahatma Gandhi? Thought he died in the forties or fifties."

"Indira Gandhi," Dane said. "The first, and so far only, female prime minister of India. She wasn't related to Mahatma. Her father was India's first prime minister. She was a very forceful ruler. She initiated a war with Pakistan and managed to wrest East Pakistan away from it; what's now known as Bangladesh. Given Bangladesh is the eighth most populous country in the world, that's historically important. Besides the fact that India is the second most populous country and a nuclear power."

Neeley nodded. "She's a world leader. Important. All right. Got it. And she's assassinated on 31 October 1984. And I'm supposed to go there and just let that happen?"

"You're supposed to insure it happens," Dane said. "There is a difference. Because it's very likely the Shadow will try to prevent the assassination."

"I'm usually the one doing the shooting," Neeley said. She held up the dagger. "Do I get more weapons than this, since I'll be around a lot of guns?"

Dane nodded. "Yes. After the brief, tell them in the ready room what you want. They have to be time period appropriate, so 1984 or earlier. And remember, you have to appear innocuous."

"Who killed her?" Neeley asked.

45

"Two of her Sikh bodyguards," Dane said. "They were retaliating after the Indian Army attacked a Sikh temple. You'll get all the pertinent details in your download. I assume Roland told you about the download?"

"You assume wrong," Neeley said. "Roland hasn't told me a thing about the Time Patrol. All I know is what I've been exposed to."

Edith stepped in. "You'll get a direct download into your memory of all the pertinent data for your mission and a sketch of data for the rest of the team's missions."

"Why am I getting info on their missions?" Neeley asked. "In fact, why am I sitting in on their mission briefings? Shouldn't this be compartmentalized?"

"You're all going to bubbles in time that exist at the same moment," Edith explained. "We've learned that sometimes one mission might possibly affect another. That happened on Independence Day. And on the last mission—" she fell silent.

"We all ended up in the same place," Roland told Neeley. "We all got diverted to Chicago where Ivar was."

"How'd that happen?" Neeley asked.

"The Shadow opened Gates in the other missions," Dane said, "and they had no choice but to go through."

"I was unconscious," Roland quickly said, blushing deeply.

"Two naked chicks tried to seduce him and get him in the Gate," Scout added.

"They weren't completely naked," Roland protested.

Scout ignored him. "But he wouldn't have any of it, so they had to knock him out. He's a good man, your Roland."

"You let yourself get knocked out?" Neeley said, as if that were a worse fate than two-naked-chicks-seduction.

"All right, all right," Dane said. "Let's move forward, not backward."

"Until we travel backward," Scout added.

Neeley held up a hand. "What happens if in this Choice thing, I don't decide to move forward with the team?"

"We'll deal with that if it happens," Dane said. He wrote:

1941

"Roland. The North Atlantic far off the coast of Iceland. You'll be on the US Navy destroyer *Reuben James*. The first American warship sunk in World War II."

"Wait a second," Eagle said. "We weren't even at war yet in October 1941. It's another five weeks until Pearl Harbor."

"We might as well have been," Dane said. "FDR had Lend-Lease passed in March of that year, which ended any pretense at neutrality on the part of the United States. The US Navy was escorting convoys to a line south of Iceland.

"The captain of the U-Boat that sank her didn't know she was American. The American escort ships were further east than the usual hand-off point for Lend-Lease convoys. The *James* was torpedoed in the early hours of the morning. Over one hundred of the one hundred and forty-four on board were lost."

Roland had been playing with his knife after the embarrassing comments by Scout, but he stopped. "What am I supposed to do? Make sure the ship sinks?"

"We don't know exactly," Dane said.

"Right." Of all the team, Roland was always the one who most easily accepted the 'vagaries of the variables' as Dane liked to call it.

"One interesting thing," Edith said. "There were seven officers and one hundred and thirty-six enlisted on board. And one passenger. I have not been able to discover who that passenger was. And if he, or she, but most likely a he, was among the survivors. None of the officers survived."

"So this passenger could be important?" Roland said.

"It's a loose end," Dane said. "The sinking of the *James*, while it caused an outcry in the United States, wasn't enough for us to declare war on Germany. It was Pearl Harbor before the U.S. declared war. So if it doesn't sink, we're not sure of the implications. Not that it matters. It was sunk, so it will sink."

"With Roland on it?" Neeley asked.

"Of course not," Dane said.

"Don't worry," Roland said to Neeley. "The missions are always like this."

"That's not reassuring," Neeley said. "Plus you're a rock in the water. You barely passed survival swimming. You wouldn't even get in the surf just now on vacation."

"You were on vacation?" Scout said.

"I don't like the water," Roland agreed, ignoring Scout. "But it won't come to that."

"Optimism," Scout said. "I like that."

"Isn't there a song about it?" Roland asked. "My bunk mate in the Ranger Battalion used to play something with Reuben James in it all the time."

Edith responded. "There is a country song with that title that was popular in the late 70's. But it has nothing to do with this. However, there is another song, by Woody Guthrie, about the sinking of the *Reuben James*."

"What about the convoy the *James* was protecting?" Eagle asked. "Could that be the key?"

"In the download, Roland will get a listing of all the ships in the HX 156 convoy and what their cargoes were," Edith said.

Dane moved on:

1828

"Shaka Zulu," Eagle said.

"Exactly," Dane confirmed. He turned to Edith, as he always did when history was in question.

"Many myths have arisen about Shaka Zulu," Edith said. "The exact date of his death is unknown although we're pretty sure on the year. The best accepted version is that he was assassinated and his body dumped in a hole and covered with dirt and stones. No one knows where he was buried. His half-brother who was part of the trio that killed Shaka, took over. He purged Shaka's closest followers and consolidated power."

"But we have no clue why I'm going on this particular day?" Eagle asked. "Nothing historically significant about it and Shaka or the Zulus? Is this the day he was killed?"

Roland tried out some of his knowledge. "Wasn't there a big battle with the Zulus? And the Brits in Redcoats? I saw the movie. It was pretty awesome."

"There was," Edith acknowledged. "The British suffered one of their greatest colonial defeats at the hands of the Zulus, but it was in 1879 at Isandlwana. And one of their greatest stands was at Rorke's Drift during the same campaign."

"That was fifty-one years later," Dane said to keep them on track.

Eagle shook his head. "Shaka was at the end of his reign if not already dead when I go. What could happen? He stays alive? Either way, his legacy is questionable. He was responsible for the *Mfecane*. The *Crushing*."

"Actually," Edith said, "a king of the Matabele tribe, after Shaka's reign, is given most of the blame for the *Mfecane*."

"Yes," Eagle said, "but Shaka started it. A domino effect. He began conquering his neighbors, The smarter of them started moving in the opposite direction, invading their neighbors. The ripple completely unbalanced the region. Millions died from starvation and war."

"Shaka's mother died in 1827," Edith said. "He went a bit crazy after that. He killed thousands. If he didn't think someone was appearing to grieve deeply enough, he had them executed."

"That's a bit harsh," Roland said.

"He was very attached to his mother," Edith understated. "He also grew up with a rather large chip on his shoulder given he was a bastard. The thing I'd worry about," Edith said, her eyes on Eagle, "is that Shaka's grip on reality wasn't the greatest in the last year of his reign. Not many missed him after he was assassinated."

"Got it," Eagle said.

"And before you ask," Dane interjected, "no, we don't have any more specifics on your mission. Shaka might already be dead by 31 October."

"All right," Eagle said, ceding to the lack of information.

"Monsters," Scout said.

"What?" Dane said.

"Monsters," she repeated. She pointed at Lara. "Tell them what you heard."

"It was just a voice," Lara said, her voice low. "In the Pit. Out of the Pit, I guess."

"What did it say?" Moms asked.

"*'Here there be monsters',*" Lara said.

"The empty spaces on old maps," Eagle said. "Do you know whose voice it was? You heard us singing on the last mission and that allowed you to help us. So there has to be a reason you heard this."

Lara shrugged. "Just some guy's voice. Clear as anything out of all the babble in the Pit. Just the one line. Like he was talking to me."

"It's a warning," Scout said. "This mission is on Halloween. Makes sense. And we've run into monsters before."

"Grendels and Aglaeca," Roland said.

"Yeti and other things," Moms added.

"A chimera in Greece," Scout said.

"I saw kraken," Neeley said. "In the Bermuda Triangle."

"Maybe the voice was the Ones Before," Scout suggested. "Warning us."

Moms spoke up. "We have to use our imaginations on these missions, given the vagaries of the variables, as Dane likes to say. But we can't let our imaginations get the better of us. Once you're on the ground, you have to quickly evaluate the situation. Look for the threat. Remember, it could be a threat to the timeline or a threat to you. Or both. Last mission, the Shadow went after us."

"Actually," Scout said, "it wanted the *entire* Time Patrol not just us. It wanted this location. And if we couldn't give it that, which we can't," she added, with a glance at Dane, "it wanted the location of the Hub we use to get here."

"Good point," Eagle said. He turned to Edith. "You can download information, but you said you could also compartmentalize and block off certain information in our brains. Can you do that with the location of the Gate below the Met? Block that in all of us for the duration of the mission?"

Edith nodded. "Yes."

"Good idea," Dane said. "Do it before they deploy," he ordered Edith. He moved on.

1692

"I guess that's me?" Lara said when Dane finished writing the date.

"Salem. Massachusetts," Dane said.

"Okeydokey," Lara said. "And what's happening there?"

"The Salem Witch Trials," Edith said.

"Then I'm screwed," Lara said. She indicated her buzzed skull and the still visible scars crisscrossing it.

"You wear your bonnet at all times," Moms said. "In fact, put it back on now. Pretend its nailed to your head."

"They probably *will* nail it to my head," Lara said.

"Do you float?" Eagle asked.

Scout was the only one who got it and, despite the circumstances, burst out laughing.

"Wood burns and wood floats," Scout said. "Like non-witches."

"Someone wanna let me in?" Lara asked.

"It's from Monty Python and *The Search for the Holy Grail*," Scout explained. "It's complicated."

"Okay," Lara said. "You'll have to fill me in if we get back."

"We'll watch it," Scout promised, "once we finish *Buffy*."

"When we get back," Eagle corrected.

"Right," Lara said. "When. That's what I meant. So what happens on Halloween in Salem? Someone get burned at the stake?"

"I could find nothing of significance on the 31st of October 1692," Edith said. "No one was burned at the stake in Salem. Actually, the worst of it was done by then. The last hangings occurred in late September. More people were arrested, but eventually almost all were released and pardoned. Two days before, on the 29th of October, the Governor had dissolved the court overseeing the trials. Eventually that State of Massachusetts would issue pardons and apologies for all those indicted."

"Oops, we hanged you by mistake?" Scout said.

"Is there a connection between Hallows Eve and witches?" Eagle asked.

"31 October is the midpoint between the Autumn Equinox and Winter Solstice," Edith said. "In the Wiccan Calendar it's known as the day when God dies to be reborn on the Winter Solstice. They believe it's the day when the line between the living and the dead is the thinnest. A time for remembrance of the dead. But, you have to understand that none of those people in Salem were really witches. It was a case of mass hysteria that got out of hand."

"So," Lara said, "no clue why I'm going on that date."

"I think Scout had a good point," Eagle said. "About the voice Lara heard and Halloween. It's too much of a coincidence. I don't believe in them."

"Nada didn't either," Scout threw in.

"Let's not just think in terms of the actual monsters the Shadow has made and sent into our timeline," Eagle said. "The Grendels and such. Valkyries were viewed as angels by those who encountered them. And the Fates certainly are not in the norm."

"The Fates aren't with the Shadow," Dane said.

"Are we certain?" Eagle said. "They were pretty involved in this last mission."

"The 'Fates'?" Neeley asked.

"He *really* doesn't tell you anything," Scout marveled.

The door opened and Sin Fen came in. She nodded at Neeley, who she'd met before. Dane handed her the chalk. "Perfect timing."

"Right," Scout said.

Sin Fen looked her in the eyes and Scout smiled. The two remained like that for a moment, then Sin Fen returned the smile. Scout nodded slightly and Sin Fen wrote on the board as she said, "This is yours, Ivar."

ZERO DAY—ZERO YEAR.   60 HUDSON STREET, NEW YORK, NY

"Zero Day," Sin Fen said, "is a term programmers use."

"I know what a Zero Day is," Ivar said. "What the hell is a Zero Year? If you don't patch a breach in a program for a year, then—" he just shook his head.

"That we don't know exactly," Sin Fen said. "It's obviously the year you're going to. The rest of the team will get the definition of Zero Day and more in the download. This address is in the lower west side of Manhattan, less than ten blocks from the World Trade Center. It was originally the Western Union Building. On the ninth floor, it houses one of the most critical Internet hubs in the world."

"Back up," Ivar said. "So this Zero Day is 31 October in some year in the past, but we don't know the year?"

"It has to be relatively recent," Sin Fen said. "After all, Scout was there when the first Internet message was sent in 1969. We're thinking it's more recent than that because the address became the hub until after Western Union was bought out in 1976. And it took a while for things to consolidate. Our best estimate is this Zero Year is some time in the last twenty years."

"We think it might be 1999," Dane said.

Ivar got that. "Leading to Y2K?"

"Perhaps," Sin Fen said. "We assume that the Shadow is going to find and exploit a Zero Day in some program on a 31 October. It's exactly two months prior to the end of the year so if it is 1999 that gives some leeway for some virus to be inserted and then spread."

"But why go to the hub on Hudson Street to do that?" Ivar asked. "You can access the Internet from anywhere. Is this why you had my computers shot?"

"Perhaps a bit of an over-reaction," Dane allowed. "But when one of the missions was pointing directly at an Internet attack, the concern was that a virus might already be in the system."

"Okay," Ivar said. "But not if the bubble isn't open yet."

"But if you fail on your mission," Dane said, "then it's here. Now."

Everyone in the room processed that for a few seconds; most sort of understood, but Roland looked at Neeley and shook his head. She shrugged and shook her head. *Not important* she mouthed to him.

"Back to my question," Ivar said. "Why go to Hudson Street?"

"We're not sure," Sin Fen said. "It might be a hardware issue. The Shadow could be trying to do something on the ninth floor."

"That's two different things," Ivar said. "Software, yeah, I can deal with that. But a physical attack? That's not my area. That's more Roland or Eagle or Moms."

"You've had training," Moms said.

Dane checked his watch. "We have a little bit of time before the bubbles open. Some of you might want additional gear. Neeley you also need to meet with Sin Fen. And Moms," he indicated the team leader, "I know you want a moment."

Dane and Edith left the team room, leaving the seven behind.

Moms awkwardly turned the wheelchair, leg poking out. "I'm not going to give the speech. You've all got things you need to do and the clock is ticking. Eagle, help Edith get Neeley up to speed on how this works and doesn't work; that is after she meets with Sin Fen.

"Make sure those of you up-arming get what you need. You'll get the cross-load on each other's mission, so that's important. Pay attention." She looked like she wanted to keep talking but couldn't find more words.

"We'll be fine," Eagle said.

"I'm sorry I'm not going," Moms said.

"You got shot," Scout said. "It's a better excuse than the dog ate my homework."

"You'll have our backs here," Eagle said. "Lara helped us out last time when she stayed behind. So there's a chance you're going to be involved."

Moms could only nod as the team headed out, leaving her alone in the team room. She looked down and noticed that her hands were twitching.

*****

"I understand this situation is exacerbated by the pending mission," Sin Fen said to Neeley.

"No shit," Neeley said. She was loading bullets into a magazine for a .45 caliber M1911 pistol. She'd chosen the venerable side arm to take along with the Naga dagger.

They were in Neeley's ready room, one door leading back to the team room, one door leading to the Gate through which she'd go to her bubble in time.

Sin Fen spoke quickly, aware of the time pressure. "In a timeline there are billion of lives. The reality is that few of those lives make a significant impact on the timeline."

"Indira Gandhi's did," Neeley said.

"Indeed she did and that is why the Shadow is trying to interfere on the day of her assassination," Sin Fen said. "But for most people, their lives will hardly cause a ripple in the timeline if something changes."

Neeley cut to the chase. "You're saying my life isn't that important."

"If any of the vast majority of people in a timeline never existed, the course of history wouldn't change. It is not a value judgment on that person or the life they live. To those who are close to them, those they love and who love them, they have a great impact."

"I've got two people I love," Neeley said. "And—"

Sin Fen interrupted. "You have Roland, who is here, and you have Hannah. You saved Hannah's life and she saved yours. That is a strong bond. But you have loved more than two people in your life."

Neeley slid the loaded magazine into a pouch under her shirt, next to the gun. She gave Sin Fen her full attention.

"Now," Sin Fen said, "you have to make a choice. To be a member of the Time Patrol, one must be a person who will never use time travel to go back and change something for personal reasons.

"Every one of us has something in our past, some point, where we wish we had chosen differently. For most it is a moment we look back on with profound regret. And that is the reason the Choice is made up front." Sin Fen held up a long, elegant hand, the three inside fingers extended. "You must now choose one of three paths.

"The first is to do nothing. To walk away. Go back to your old life in the Cellar. However, there is a caveat to that. If you do so, we will wipe your memory of this place, of this Team. We must do so for security reasons."

"Hold on," Neeley protested. "I already knew about this place and about the Patrol."

"True," Sin Fen said. "We made that exception for Hannah and you. But now you're in further."

"If you wipe my knowledge of this place," Neeley said, "doesn't that mean you wipe my knowledge of Roland?"

"Yes."

"That ship already sailed when I said yes to coming here," Neeley said. "So forget option one."

"The second path," Sin Fen said, "is to go back to a key moment in your life and change that moment. I will tell you that moment shortly."

"I don't get to pick the moment?" Neeley asked.

"No." She smiled slightly to lessen the sting of the abrupt answer. "However, if you believe the moment I tell you is wrong, you may let me know."

"All right. Have you ever been wrong on it?"

"I don't believe so."

"So what is it?"

Sin Fen explained. "If you choose to go to that moment, we will let you go. But that will the end of you in the present. You will be in the past. You will also have no memory of how you got there except for knowledge of what is going to happen very soon in that moment. Within twenty-four hours and then you will live the rest of your live from that moment forward.

"The third path is to become a member of the Time Patrol, to accept your past completely, and go through that door to your gate and on your mission." Sin Fen waited a few seconds. "Do you understand?"

"Yes."

"There is more to your Choice than you think," Sin Fen said.

"When I was on the plane in Berlin and realized I'd been given a bomb?" Neeley said. "Or before that when--"

"No," Sin Fen said.

That gave Neeley pause. "All right. Tell me."

"The moment is when Gant was first diagnosed with cancer and was told it was treatable," Sin Fen said. "But he knew if he got treatment, it would lead enemies to the two of you. So he did nothing. He didn't tell you about the cancer until it was too late. It was months before you were even aware he was sick even though you were living together at the time."

Neeley took a step back, exhaling as if punched in the chest. "I didn't know."

"That was his intent," Sin Fen said. "You could go back to the day he found out, but didn't tell you. When he walked in the door of the cabin in Vermont and told you everything was fine. Perhaps you could convince him to get treatment?"

Neeley took a deep breath. She pulled the .45 out, pulled the slide back, chambering a round. She put it back in the concealed holster.

"Then I have to honor his intent."

Neeley went to the door leading to her gate.

*****

"You're a tall drink of water," Angus said as Edith Frobish approached.

"Be polite," Orlando warned.

"When am I not?" Angus seemed to honestly want an answer.

They were in the Metropolitan Museum of Art, in one of the most recent rotating exhibits. After closing, there was only the soft sound of air circulating through the large vents and Edith's short heels clicking on the floor as she walked up.

"I'm Edith Frobish," she said, extending her hand.

Instead of shaking her hand, Angus gently took it in his own and bowed, kissing the back of it. "The pleasure is all mine. I'm Angus. I'd give you my surname and my clan's entire lineage, but a man must save some information for further conversation with a beautiful woman. You can't be knowing all my secrets at once."

Edith blushed.

"He's a rogue," Orlando said. "And not in the good way."

Angus indicated the exhibition, a series of paintings of random patterns in stark black and white. "This is art?"

"It is," Edith said.

"It is beyond my ken to appreciate," Angus said.

Edith looked at the paintings. "To be honest, I don't understand why some of it makes it in here, even though it's my area of expertise."

Angus indicated Orlando. "Why would a pretty lass with an interest in art be affiliated with a ruffian like this? And he be a ruffian not in the good way."

"Art records history," Edith said. "Would you come with me?"

"This is where we part ways," Orlando said to Angus.

"Until we meet again," Angus said.

"Until we meet again." Orlando held out his hand.

Angus shook it, but Orlando laughed. "Nice try. My flask?"

"Ah!" Angus pulled it out and handed it over. "Upgrade your tastes, my friend."

"It gets the job done." Orlando nodded at both of them and then walked off.

"I worry about him," Edith said. "He's always half-drunk."

"Don't be," Angus said. "And he's not half-drunk. He's drunk. Think of it as his medicine."

"What ails him?"

"That be his business," Angus said. "Now where we be going?"

Edith led the way through a door painted to look like part of a wall. They were into the back corridors of the Met. "I assume Colonel Orlando didn't tell you why we've recruited you?"

"It won't be for art appreciation," Angus said. "I would assume, knowing Orlando as I do, that has something to do with nefarious activities of the covert kind."

"You're here to be assessed as a potential member of the Time Patrol."

"You're off your head, lass."

"I'm afraid not."

"Well, then, let's be at it."

The Missions Phase I

"By their nature, computer systems bring together a series of vulnerabilities: accidental disclosures, deliberate penetrations, and physical attack."
WILLIS WARE: 1967 Security Reports for Computer
Systems
ZERO DAY; ZERO YEAR

IVAR WASN'T THERE, and then he was there, but he'd sort of always been there. It was the best way to explain how he arrived, becoming part of his current time and place without fanfare or excitement among those around him.

The only problem was he didn't know exactly where 'there' was right away, and he wasn't sure 'when' this was. Is. Whatever.

He was standing in the midst of low bushes next to a flagpole. The bushes were inside a waist-high black, metal fence, inside a park, and there was no doubt where the park was: New York City. The sound of traffic, and the towering buildings surrounding the park confirmed that since there is no place quite like the Big Apple, plus it was his designated destination.

He looked down. The stone at the base of the flagpole read: DUANE PARK.

The download dumped data, orienting him and momentarily overwhelming: the first public space acquired by the City for a park, starting in 1797, yada, yada, Ivar cut off the download, happy to at least know where exactly he was. It made sense, because when he turned to the northeast, diagonally across, there was 60 Hudson Street.

"Close enough," Ivar muttered. He carefully stepped on several walking stones and made it to the sidewalk. It was night, actually early morning, but New York is the City That Never Sleeps, and there was the occasional cab or car zipping by.

Ivar counted floors on 60 Hudson. The ninth floor was dimly lit, but that was because the windows were mostly shuttered on the inside, to bolster the cooling needed for the machinery. There was no night or day inside that floor as it connected to the entire world.

Ivar froze as he felt something prod into his lower back. "Frak me," he muttered.

"How are the Alps in May?" a low voice asked.

"I'm sure they're fine," Ivar said.

"Tsk-tsk. Wrong answer."

"I'm just out for a walk," Ivar said. "You can have my wallet. My watch. Whatever you want." He knew the man wasn't holding a gun on him for his wallet; plus he didn't have one. Or a watch. He realized the question had been a form of bona fides, where he was supposed to supply the right answer. Except he hadn't been briefed on any bona fides or that someone was waiting for him.

"Most interesting," the person holding the gun said. "If we had not been watching with thermals, I don't think we would have picked you up.

Ivar slowly looked over his shoulder. A man wearing a nice suit was behind him. His skin was well tanned, skull shaved, but his eyes were black, and had the look Ivar had seen too many times: a killer.

The man took a step back. "You may not be my contact, but you are someone arriving most uniquely, so I must pursue this further. Let us be professionals, shall we not?"

"We shall," Ivar said, running that through his head for a second, belatedly trying to figure out if he'd just agreed or disagreed.

"This is a bit public," the man said. "Shall we discuss this in a place more private?"

"I like public," Ivar said.

The gun indicated for him to move. "What you like is not significant under the circumstances."

It is Now. Zero Day in Zero Year. How we got to be here via the computer timeline?

59

1937: Professor Atanasoff of Iowa State University tries to build a computer without gears, cams, belts or shafts.

1941: Atanasoff designs a computer that can solve 29 equations simultaneously, which is also the first time a computer can store information in a memory.

1943-1944: Two University of Pennsylvania Professors build the Electronic Numerical Integrator and Calculator (ENIAC), but it takes six women (ENIAC Six) to figure out how to program and maintain its over 18,000 vacuum tubes and they survive to do that (thanks to Moms savings their lives).

1946: The same two professors build UNIVAC for the Census Bureau, the first commercial computer (previous ones had been military).

1947: William Shockley and two other invent the transistor, allowing vacuum tubes to be replaced by a solid electric switch.

1953: Grace Hopper invents COBOL, the first computer language.

1954: FORTRAN is invented for programming.

1958: The first computer chip is invented.

1964: Douglas Engelbart unveils a prototype of the modern computer using a mouse and a graphical use interface.

1969: Bell Labs releases UNIX, an operating system that makes computers compatible.

1969: The first Internet message is sent from UCLA to Stanford consisting of two letters before the system crashes, but it was sent (thanks to Scout).

Ivar allowed himself to directed toward a Fedex Home Delivery van parked on Hudson Street. As they came up to it, the back door swung open and he was shoved in.

"What do we have?" the man who opened the door asked. He was fat, dressed in a Fedex uniform with food stains on the front, and had a thin sheen of hair desperately combed over his balding scalp. "That the person you're supposed to meet?"

"Sit in the corner, on the floor," the gunman ordered Ivar.

Ivar did so, wondering why his missions always started out under threat. He'd heard the debriefs. The others always didn't start that way, although they always ended up under threat.

Some things change; some don't.

"You just appeared out of nothing," the gunman said. "One second there is no one in the park, then there is you. That is most strange. Would you not agree?"

"You mean would I agree?" Ivar was getting tired of the twisted language.

"Indeed."

"I was just out for a walk," Ivar said.

"Are you not a professional?" the man asked.

The Fedex guy had a large pizza box open on a console facing an array of displays. They were showing ambient light, thermal and night vision images of the surrounding area, but mostly 60 Hudson. Some of them were scrolling data; very quickly.

"Are you the mob?" Ivar asked, figuring the odds, his odds at least, were good on that account.

Gunman looked at Fedex man. "Are we the mob?"

"Can I be Tony Soprano?" Fedex guy asked.

"You may not," Gunman said. "You might though, be Big Pussy Bonpensiero."

Fedex guy laughed. "What's that make you?"

Gunman pondered the question. "I do not believe I would fit in that show. I'm a professional." He shifted his attention back to Ivar. "Your inexperience and your questions indicate you are not the person I was supposed to meet.

Fedex guy turned serious. "What are we gonna do with him?" He had a New York accent.

But Ivar couldn't place Gunman's accent.

"I'm afraid *we're* not going to do anything with him," Gunman said.

"Huh?" Fedex guy grunted as he picked up another slice of pizza.

Gunman fired, the suppressed pistol making a rather loud noise in the confines of the van. The bullet hit Fedex in left eye. There was no exit wound as the modified .22 caliber shell spread shards through his brain, shredding it.

The slice hit the floor with a splat. Fedex man slumped in the seat.

"No double-tap?" Ivar asked, trying to remain calm.

"No need, as you can clearly see."

"Right. I was taught double-tap."

"You were taught correctly," Gunman said, "but situations differ." He waggled the gun, which was now pointed, more or less, but more, at Ivar. "Twenty-two High Standard. A classic. One shot, eyeball, is enough. But you must be very accurate. The eye socket is a small target."

"Right." Ivar swallowed. "And now?"

"'And now'?" He seemed to realize something. "Excuse me. I have failed to introduce myself. I am Victor."

"'Victor'?" Ivar nodded. "Sure. Victor. I'm Ivar."

"You are not my contact, but I strongly suspect you are involved in this matter," Victor said.

"What matter is that?" Ivar asked.

"We had an incident a while back. In the Negev."

This was worse than the mob, Ivar realized. *The fraking Israelis.*

"Someone appeared. Like you did. Caused great damage. I read the report and watched the surveillance tapes." He pointed the pistol with the stubby suppressor directly at Ivar's left eye. "Who are you and how did you get here?"

"I need no bodyguard at all, for even the bravest men who approach me get weak at the knees and their hearts turn to water." Shaka Zulu
Zululand, Africa, 31 October 1828 A.D.

EAGLE WASN'T THERE, and then he was there, but he'd sort of always been there. It was the best way to explain how he arrived, becoming part of his current time and place without fanfare or excitement among those around him. But not without notice, as there was another person on top of the small knoll. However that person expressed, as noted, no fanfare or excitement. He was seated on a makeshift throne overlooking the surrounding jungle.

"I did not believe the witch," Shaka Zulu said, "but I thought it best to humor her, because there are times when the demons do line up behind a witch's prophecies."

It was night, the clearing on top of the knoll was about thirty feet wide, surrounded by—Eagle blinked, realizing it wasn't trees all about, but tall stakes, roughly fifteen feet high. And a person was impaled on each. They were so many and so close together, it was easy to mistake for jungle in the dark.

The odor in the air was of blood, voided bowels and the unmistakable stench of death with the impaled in various stages of decomposition. There was an occasional moan, indicating not all the victims were dead. As his eyes adjusted, Eagle could make out more detail. Two in the closest row, a man and woman, had their hands clasped in the space between their stakes. She was dead, but his chest was moving, very slightly, and he still gripped her hand.

It is 1828. French explorer Rene Caillie becomes the first 'infidel' to go to Timbuktu and come out alive; a typhoon kills an estimated 10,000 in Kyushu, Japan; the world's population is just over a billion of which about 12 million live in the United States; Andrew Jackson's wife, Rachel, dies less than a month after he is elected President; 32,000 slaves from Angola are sold in Rio de Janiero, Brazil; Jules Verne is born; Joshua Chamberlain, who would save the Union at Gettysburg, is born; chocolate milk powder is patented; Leo Tolstoy, who would write some books, is born.

There was a body staked down, spread-eagle in front of the King. An old woman.

Some things change, some don't.

"Should I let you live, witch?" Shaka asked her as he stood. He was of medium height, not exactly imposing. But he had an aura that was perceptible; of course the death and suffering all around at his order was more than perceptible.

Shaka had dark brown skin and was dressed similar to Eagle. Unlike many Zulu kings who would follow, he was not fat, but well muscled. However, his nose was too big and he had a scar running from above his right eye along his scalp. He held an *iklwa* in his right hand, the metal glinting in the moonlight.

Eagle realized the throne Shaka had been seated upon was made of animal skins over bones tied together with sinew. Human bones. That had to be pretty uncomfortable, Eagle thought.

"My words are true," the old woman said, her voice dry and cracking. "You see the apparition in front of you as I foretold."

"Does the apparition speak?" Shaka pointed his *iklwa* at Eagle.

"I speak, great King." Eagle, always proficient with languages, was having no trouble using the download of Zulu, a sub-tongue of Bantu.

"The witch says you come from far away," Shaka said, "yet you dress like one of my warriors. So you are a spy?"

"I am not a spy, great King."

"If you were a spy, of course you would say you are not a spy," Shaka said. "There has never been a spy who admitted he was a spy. Until the pain became so great. Then they all finally admit."

"A man will admit to anything under great pain, King."

"Because if I say they are a spy, then they are a spy," Shaka said. "They should not have wasted my time lying."

A voice cried out from the forest of the impaled, begging for the mercy of death. Shaka smiled, displaying two prominent front teeth. "A brave man does not beg."

Dying men did. Eagle had heard very brave men cry out when mortally wounded. For God, for their mothers, for a quick ending.

"Your words have come true," Shaka said, prodding the old woman with the tip of the *iklwa*. "Three prophecies, three truths. Is there anything more to your prophecy than you have told me?"

The old woman was silent. For too long as Shaka jabbed her with the short spear, breaking skin. "Tell me."

"I would need time for more prophecy, my King. To look with my Sight." At the last word she turned her head to look at Eagle. Her eyes implored him to help her.

"If you have no more prophecies," Shaka said, "you have no more time."

"But, my King! My words were true!"

"That means you are a true witch," Shaka reasoned. "And should die."

Before Eagle could react, Shaka slammed the *iklwa* into the old woman's chest, pinning her to the ground. She squirmed for a few moments, then went still. He pulled it out and Eagle understood that the weapon was indeed named for the noise it coming back out of a body. But the metal was too smooth, too shiny. Eagle realized it was also made of Naga metal.

"Come here, spy," Shaka said, gesturing for Eagle to come to his throne. "There is something I want to show you. Perhaps in your treasonous life, you have seen something like it." Eagle knew he stood no chance against Shaka *iklwa* to *iklwa*.

He walked forward, stepping around the dead witch.

Shaka leaned his *iklwa* against the throne made of the bones of his vanquished. He reached down and tossed an object toward Eagle. It thudded to the ground and rolled once.

The hairless head was covered in dark green scales. The forehead sloped sharply back. The eyes were deep set, so far back in the sockets, they were barely visible. The wide mouth hung open, revealing razor-sharp teeth and four large fangs.

"What is that?" Shaka demanded.

Eagle knew why he was here. "That, great King, is the head of a mighty beast we call a Grendel. And if there is one, there is at least one more like it. Larger, more dangerous. Capable of bearing many, many more."

Shaka laughed, a crazy edge to it. "At least *one* more? As the witch prophesized, in the Valley of Death to the west. There are dozens of these beasts, guarding a watering hole. It was a mighty fight to get this one head. They were sent here to torment me in my grief."

"A man may think God sleeps, but God sees everything, I know it now."
Arthur Miller, *The Crucible*
Salem Massachusetts, 31 October 1692 A.D.

LARA WASN'T THERE, and then she was there, but she'd sort of always been there. It was the best way to explain how she arrived, becoming part of her current time and place without fanfare or excitement among those around her, because there wasn't anyone around her.

Except, of course, for Pandora, who was very aware of her sudden arrival out of time.

"Oh, you're new," Pandora greeted her with disappointment. "I was expecting Scout."

Lara didn't respond. She was taking in her surroundings as this was her first Time Patrol mission to a specific date in the timeline and not to the Space Between. She was in a forest clearing, hopefully on the outskirts of Salem, Massachusetts. Night. A quarter moon.

And a disreputable 'goddess' of myth.

"You must be Lara," Pandora said. She was tall, dressed in a white robe. Her hair was jet black except for a single streak of silver that began above her left eye and over her shoulder. She had a Naga staff in hand, with the seven-headed snake haft on the ground, the sharp end pointing up.

Lara finally acknowledged Pandora. "Scout says you're not much help. Actually, she says you're a pain in the ass."

Pandora was offended. "I helped Scout. Let me recall when. Ah. Yes. It was 480 B.C.. I assisted her in defeating a Legion. Xerxes' Dagger he was called although one should never given things formal names. A very formidable opponent. One who, untested and unprepared as Scout was, she would not have survived without my assistance. You may tell Scout, if you see her again, her words wound me."

"So what are you here for?" Lara asked.

"Same thing as you," Pandora said.

A long silence played out.

"You don't know why you're here, do you?" Pandora asked.

"They've already hung all they're gonna hang," Lara said.

"Hanged," Pandora said. "Things are hung. People are hanged."

Lara continued. "I'm figuring they're planning on hunging someone else and they aren't supposed to do that."

"Cute." Pandora sighed. "If things were only that simple."

"Scout also said you weren't a font of information." Lara didn't like this forest. It was pitch black under the surrounding trees. A narrow trail ran from one end of the clearing and disappeared into the darkness on the other end. She didn't know which way Salem lay. Lie. Whatever.

"A 'font' or a 'fount'?" Pandora asked. "Language usage has changed over the centuries."

"She threw in that you weren't funny," Lara said. "Why are *you* here?"

"Because you're here," Pandora said.

"You said you were expecting Scout, so that's a lie."

"I was using a generic *'you're'*," Pandora said. "More accurately, I knew there was going to be a time bubble here and now, and I assumed one of your people would show up. I just thought it would be Scout, given the specific nature of this bubble."

"And why is that?"

"When and where did Scout go?" Pandora asked. "We could only see several of the bubbles. 31 October. We know there is one in 1941. A warship. But she wouldn't go there. That would be Roland or Eagle's province. Not to Africa either. Perhaps the killing in India?"

"So you don't know as much as you like others to think you know," Lara said.

"When did Scout go?" Pandora persisted. "Ah. I bet it is 1517. The most important mission. At least you might think so. But what is apparent isn't always so."

"Right," Lara said.

Pandora shook her head. "The Fates are meddling more and more. Your team was lucky to have survived your last mission. That twist was unexpected."

"I'd love to chat—not." Lara looked at the path.

"So, like Scout, you're clueless why you're bouncing around in time," Pandora said. "I'm surprised you people have lasted this long."

"Scout did say you were thinking Alexander Great was the One or the Two or maybe it was the Three. But he wasn't."

"Scout said a lot to you," Pandora noted. "Best friends?"

"We hang together," Lara said. "Or it is hung?"

It is 1692. A combined English and Dutch fleet defeats the French at the Battle of La Hogue; in the course of the year 20 people are hanged for witchcraft in Salem; the Massacre of Glencoe when 38 men of the Clan MacDonald are executed for not swearing an oath of allegiance to King William of England, subsequently about 40 women and children die of exposure and starvation because their homes were burned; on September 22nd the last hanging, 8 people, occurs in Salem; A slave revolt is crushed in Barbados.

Lara noted the path to the right went down slightly, while the one to the left went up. Would a village be on high ground for protection or low ground for proximity to water?

And where the frak did all that come from, Lara wondered. Maybe they put Salem wherever the frak it is because some farmer got tired of walking and thought *this looks as good as anywhere. Hell, why does anyone live in Boise?*

Some things change, some don't.

But the download intruded, informing her that Salem was located at the mouth of a river on the east coast of Massachusetts. So downhill would make more sense. Or into the rising sun, whenever that might occur. Not that she was going to hang here with this whacko broad until dawn.

"I really thought—" Pandora began, but she paused. "Do you have the Sight?"

"Sort of," Lara said.

"Do you sense him?"

Lara *did* sense something or someone. In the forest. Moving. Coming this way. She'd felt this presence before; even met it.

"Joey," she whispered.

"Who is Joey?" Pandora said, turning in the direction of the presence, lifting her Naga to the ready. "You met one before?"

"He is darkness," Lara said. "Evil."

"You do have some Sight," Pandora acknowledged. "It is Legion." She lowered the point of her Naga staff slightly. "It is going away. But it knows we're here."

"Why didn't he attack?" Lara asked. She'd drawn her Naga dagger without consciously realizing it. She had sensed more than just the Legion. There were things out there. Not human.

"It is not here for us," Pandora said.

"Who is it here for? And why are you calling him 'it'?"

"I truly expected it to be Scout that was chosen for this mission," Pandora said.

"Why is that?" Lara asked.

"Because if you fail in this mission, Scout will cease to exist."

"You cannot shake hands with a clenched first."
Prime Minister Indira Gandhi
New Delhi, India, 31 October 1984

NEELEY WASN'T THERE, and then she was there, but she'd sort of always been there. It was the best way to explain how she arrived, becoming part of her current time and place without fanfare or excitement among those around her, except for the other person in the room, who didn't raise a fuss.

"Welcome," Indira Gandhi said. "Would you like some tea? I have a pot on."

Neeley, veteran of many extreme situations though she was, needed a moment to adjust after her first time travel. She was in an alcove next to a nondescript kitchen. Prime Minister Indira Gandhi was standing eight feet away, between Neeley and the kitchen. The Prime Minister was wrapped in a robe made of khadi and was shorter than Neeley expected although the download supplied her current exact height, weight and other details that were coming from an autopsy report, which was a bit disconcerting, even for Neeley.

"Tea would be fine," Neeley said.

"Was it a long journey?" Gandhi asked as she turned and went to the stove. A kettle was already boiling, a flame beneath it. Two cups were set off to the side on a tray.

Definitely expecting company.

"It was," Neeley said.

"Would you like to sit?" Gandhi indicated a chair at a small wooden table.

Neeley understood cover for action and cover for position and felt fragile on both fronts. The first rule of Time Patrol was knocking on her consciousness, a quite irritating intrusion, as if Edith Frobish's download didn't trust Neeley.

For a moment Neeley wondered how Roland dealt with the download, then she smiled, knowing he could shut it off much easier than she could.

"Thank you," Neeley said. She sat, smoothly drawing her M1911 pistol as she did so and placing it on her lap, round in the chamber, her thumb on the safety, finger on the trigger.

"Sugar? Milk?" Indira Gandhi asked as she carefully poured boiling water into a cup.

"No, thank you," Neeley said.

Gandhi nodded. She brought the tray over and placed a cup in front of Neeley. Then got one for herself. "I did not expect a woman. That makes me very joyful."

"Yes," Neeley said, clueless about how to proceed having tea with a woman who would be dead in the morning; 9:20 a.m. to be exact.

"I am Indira. And you are?"

"Neeley, Prime Minister."

"There is no need to be formal, is there?" Gandhi asked. "Not now. Not this evening, actually very early morning as the hour has already passed midnight into a new day."

"Yes ma'am," Neeley said, not as used as her time travelling teammates to meeting historic figures.

"Indira, please. And is Neeley your first name or surname?"

"It's just my name."

Gandhi pursed her lips. "Curious. Surely you were born with a full name?"

"I was."

Gandhi held up a hand. "I sense the issue is one that is sensitive to you. Forgive my intrusion. Neeley. Most interesting. You sound American, but there is a trace of an accent in your English. Having grown up here but being schooled in Europe, I have heard many voices. A bit of French perhaps?"

"I lived there for a while," Neeley admitted, wondering if she was breaking her cover. Then again, in covert ops, always tell the truth is the best cover. Until it was time not to tell the truth.

"Ah, France," Gandhi said. "Joan d'Arc. A true hero. A woman ahead of her time." There was an excitement to her voice when she spoke. The download confirmed that Gandhi had a deep interest in Joan of Arc. Gandhi glanced down. "And you brought a gun."

Neeley put the pistol on the table. "For protection."

"Really? And you know how to use it?"

"I do."

Gandhi took a sip of tea. Neeley gingerly raised the fragile piece of porcelain to her lip with her off-hand. "This is very nice."

"My own mixture," Gandhi said. "Tea is such a strange symbol in my country. The British exploited us for it but it is still a rich export that helps drive our economy. It seems everything in life cuts both ways. Now we no longer have the British but we still have our tea." Gandhi indicated the pistol. "Will you shoot me with that?"

"No," Neeley said. "I'm not going to shoot you."

It is 1984 A.D. Terms of Endearment wins best picture at the Oscars; the AIDS virus is uncovered; the Soviet Union boycotts the summer Olympics in Los Angeles; Bruce Springsteen releases 'Born in the USA'; during a voice check, Reagan is overheard joking that the United States will begin bombing the Soviet Union in five minutes; Band Aid releases 'Do They Know It's Christmas' to help with the famine in Ethiopia; the Bhopal industrial disaster kills over 8,000 outright in India in the worst industrial accident in history; an explosion at a Russian naval base destroys 2/3rds of all their stockpiled missiles; the space shuttle Discovery *launches on its first mission; the US Embassy in Beirut is car-bombed, killing 24 people.*

"Really?" Gandhi was surprised. "Then why are you here?"

"To protect you," Neeley lied. "Why do you think you're going to be shot?"

Some things change; some don't.

"I was told I would die today," Gandhi said.

"She flew the Stars and Stripes of the land of the free
But tonight she's in her grave on the bottom of the sea."
Woody Guthrie

The North Atlantic, 31 October 1941 A.D.

ROLAND WASN'T THERE, and then he was there, but he'd sort of always been there, except he really wasn't aware he was there, because he was asleep. It was the best way to explain how he arrived, becoming part of his current time and place without fanfare or excitement among those around him, including Roland, because he along with everyone else in the berth was sleeping.

This was despite the fact the *USS Reuben James* was pitching and rolling with the North Atlantis swells. They were in a windowless berth with bunks stacked four high and a narrow space in between. Every bunk was occupied, because space was limited and with at least one third of the ship always on watch, the other two thirds was resting. This meant those coming off duty slid into what was known as a 'hot bunk'.

Roland struggled to consciousness when someone jabbed him, hard, with a finger in the shoulder. "Get up."

Roland blinked, coming alert, but disoriented not just from the travel through time, but being awoken after traveling through time, which raised the interesting question that since he hadn't been asleep when he stepped into the gate, exactly *when* had he fallen asleep since the time travel was supposed to be instantaneous?

But Roland wasn't wondering about that. He was making sure that the Naga dagger was secure in its sheath in his belt and squinting to see whether who had poked him was a threat.

All he could make out was a man dressed in what the download informed him was a 'foul weather uniform' consisting of a bulky waterproof oilskin jacket and trousers with a 'sou-wester hat'. Which meant Roland couldn't make out any details at all.

"Get dressed." The man shoved a similar set of outer garments at Roland. He spoke with an accent that Roland found oddly familiar, but couldn't place.

Roland automatically began gearing up, assuming the man was going to take the rack he was vacating, but the man made no move to take off his outer garments. Oilskin pants and jacket on, Roland followed as the man gestured. They went down the passage between bunks hanging from the ceiling—overhead, the download corrected—from chains. Roland was rocking back and forth as the ship rode the waves.

Roland didn't like being in the water, and he wasn't fond of being on water either.

The man opened a hatch and they stumbled through to a passageway. He shut the hatch behind them and then turned to face Roland.

Roland's only excuse could be the unique sleeping arrival because before he could react, the man had a blade against Roland's neck.

*It is 1941. In July, Roosevelt orders all Japanese assets seized in the US; Pearl Harbor is attacked six months later in December; in September, the State of Maine 'declares war' on Germany; Hitler orders a stop to the T4 program, but those still alive are sent to concentration camps so . . . .; the Siege of Leningrad begins and will last until 1944 with over one million civilians dying; Charles Lindbergh testifies before Congress that the US should negotiate a neutrality treaty with Germany; Lend-Lease is passed and Churchill tells the US: "*Give us the tools, and we will finish the job*"; Dumbo is released; the* Bismarck *is sunk; plutonium is discovered; Hitler breaks his neutrality with Russia and Operation Barbarossa is launched; commercial TV is authorized by the FCC; the British SAS, Special Air Service (Who Dares Wins) is formed; the slogan V For Victory is initiated by the BBC; Zyklon B is introduced at Auschwitz; the keel of the* USS Missouri *is laid at Brooklyn Navy Yard and four years later the war will end on its deck on the other side of the world; Bob Hope performs his first USO show—it will be far from his last; an Enigma machine is captured off a German U-Boat.*

"Who are you?" the man put pressure on the blade.

"Roland." Roland slowly moved his left hand toward the handle of his dagger.

"Are you friend or foe?"

Some things change, some don't.

Since Roland had no clue who this guy was, he had no clue how to answer. "Friend or foe of who?"

"I was told one out of time would come. I felt the disturbance of your arrival. Why are you here?"

Another question Roland didn't quite know how to answer. He want to Roland default mode; the truth. "To make sure everything happens as it should."

The man laughed without mirth. "What *should* happen? You know? What do you know?"

"This ship sinks."

"*This* ship sinks'?" The man was incredulous. "Who cares about *this* ship? It's the other ship, the submarine, that we have to worry about. That's the one we have to destroy."

The accent finally clicked into place in Roland's memory. "You're a Jager. Where are the Aglaeca and Grendels you're hunting?"

"You are not only responsible for what you say, but also for what you do not say."
Martin Luther
Wittenberg, Germany, 31 October 1517 A.D.

SCOUT WASN'T THERE, and then she was there, but she'd sort of always been there, but she was really tired of going to places that didn't have hot, running water. And where people were waiting to kill her. It was the best way to explain how she arrived, becoming part of her current time and place and immediately having to dodge a surprisingly slow knife thrust.

Surprisingly slow given who held the knife, that is.

Her training, muscle memory, and the Sight saved her life. She was 'aware' of the attack before she was consciously aware of her surroundings. She whirled away from the thrust, drawing her Naga dagger and assumed a defensive position. She was in a cathedral, dimly lit by sputtering candles; good lighting also lacking in places with no hot, running water.

Her opponent was as surprised by his lethargic attack as much as she.

"Do not interfere!" he screamed.

"Who you talking to?" Scout asked, her eyes adjusting. He was of average height, average build, dressed in black pants, tunic and with a black scarf across the lower half of his face—he was Legion; seen one, seen them all it seemed.

"The old bitch," Legion said, adjusting his position, getting ready for a real fight since the ambush had failed

"Fate?" Scout asked. "Or Pandora?"

"You reacted well," Legion said. "What is your name? Are you the one they call Moms?"

"Do I look like a Moms?" Scout asked.

"Scout then. Your blood will be sweet on my blade."

73

"Seriously?" Scout said. "Did you make that up or do you guys study saying crap like that? Do you have a script? Do you practice in front of a mirror?"

He came at her and once more, she was surprised how slow he was, although it was quicker than the previous attack, as fast as a normal person. However, Legion were anything but normal. She was able to parry his thrust, his secondary thrust, and, being Legion, the third backslash, all done in one, continuous flow.

"This is not fair!" he called out, not quite as vigorously as before.

"Who else is here?" Scout asked, not daring to take her eyes off him, because if he got exponentially faster, up to full speed, she was going to be in trouble. Of course—

He came in dagger held high, then unexpectedly dropped, sliding along the marble floor. Scout narrowly avoided having the artery on the inside of her thigh sliced open. She escaped with only a shallow slice just above the knee as she threw herself up and to the left, tumbling, hitting the hard floor. She took the landing on the flat of the back of her shoulder as trained and rolled over, spinning about, coming to her feet at the ready.

"Now it's fair."

The voice echoed in the cathedral. Dry, cracking at the edges, female, at a conversational level. Not particularly interested in what was developing, other than to make the observation. Not Pandora—Scout knew her voice.

Scout shut out her worry about whose voice it was. Shut out everything but the man in front of her. The threat. The blade. Her own blade.

And time. Most of all time.

Legion drew a second dagger, a concession to upgraded respect for his opponent. Scout shifted her feet, adjusting.

Legion put one blade to his lips and licked it. "Your blood is indeed sweet. Are you a virgin?"

"Are you serious? I think—" and she darted to her right, jumping onto a pew, and continuing up into the air.

No one ever looks up, Nada had always preached.

Scout's Naga dagger drew a thin red line along the side of his scalp starting at the temple, slicing through his ear, and ending at the back of the neck.

Scout landed on her feet. "That was pretty cool. Didn't know I could do that."

It is 1517 A.D. The world's population is roughly half a billion people; Grand Prince Vasili III of Muscovy conquers Ryazan; Maria of Aragon, Queen of Portugal, dies; Sir Thomas Pert reaches Hudson Bay; the first burning at the stake of Protestants in the Netherlands (it won't be the last).

Legion turned to face her. No pain evident on his face, although blood seeped from the wound, particularly the split ear.

Some things change; some don't.

"Do you think this is fair?" Scout called out to the unknown voice. She took a step back and addressed Legion. "Are you here for Luther?"

"I am here for you," he said.

"Lucky me."

"And then Luther."

"Unlucky you," Scout said.

Legion called out to the unknown observer once more. "You must let this play out."

There was a dry chuckle. "'Must'? Who are you to tell me what I must do? But, I have stopped interfering, as you call it. The fight is between the two of you."

Legion took a step back. "That was you?" he said to Scout.

"You got it," Scout said.

"That should not be," Legion muttered.

Scout saw the moment of doubt in his eyes and attacked, feinting for the face, then slamming the point into his chest. He was too shocked to use his blades, even though she was pressed up against him.

"Someone once told me there's only two types of knife fighters," Scout said. "The quick and the dead. That's a Nada Yada." She twisted the blade, shredding Legion's heart. She watched the life go out of his eyes, then let him slide off her blade.

The Possibility Palace

"In a timeline there are billion of lives," Sin Fen said. "The reality is that few of those lives make a significant impact on the timeline."

"Ya think?" Angus said. "We're all just wee little specks of sand on a big beach. Some getting washed up, some getting washed away, most getting tumbled about aimlessly but overall, it doesn't matter, does it now, lass?" He pointed into the Pit. "This pretty much says that, does it not?"

"It does," Sin Fen agreed. The two were alone on the spiral ramp, not far from the door to the team room. "If any of the vast majority of people in a timeline never existed, the course of history wouldn't change. It is not a value judgment on that person or the life they live. To those who are close to them, those they love and who love them, they have a great impact."

"Are you gonna tell me something I don't know?" Angus asked, not with anger or frustration, but with curiosity.

"I'm telling what I've told every prospective member of the Time Patrol," Sin Fen said. "A preamble to a question."

"Be getting to the quick of it," Angus said.

"You have to make a Choice," Sin Fen said. "To be a member of the Time Patrol, one must be a person who will never use time travel to go back and change something for personal reasons. Every one of us has something in our past, some point, where we wish we had chosen differently. For many it is a moment we look back on with profound regret."

"I've got no regrets," Angus said.

"Everyone has regrets," Sin Fen disagreed. "Unless they are a psychopath, and you are not."

"Some might say I am seeing as I was in the Super-Max for the rest of me breathing days according to the judge who sent me there."

Sin Fen ignored that. "A team member can never use time travel for personal reasons. And that is the reason the Choice is made up front. You must now choose one of three paths. The first is to do nothing. To walk away."

"Go back to prison?"

"It is the life you came from as a result of all your previous choices."

"Let's move on to curtain number two," Angus. "Ye remember that show, don't ya?"

"If you make that first choice," Sin Fen said, "we will wipe your memory of this place, of this Team."

"Will you wipe Orlando's ugly mug too? Let's be moving on. I be intrigued now. And I won't be going back."

"The second door," Sin Fen said, "is to go back to a key moment in your life and change that moment."

"I'll go back," Angus said. "I know the exact place and time."

Sin Fen sighed. "It's a moment in *your* life. Where you were present."

Angus folded his arms over his chest. "Why not elsewhere? You be saying we can travel in time. Why can't we go wherever we want in the past? That's what this whole Time Patrol thing is about, is it not? Why is it limited to *my* life and where I was? If I'd have been there, then there'd be no regretting."

"That's the way it is," Sin Fen said.

"Lots of bugs in ya system here," Angus pointed out.

"We're doing the best we can. If you chose to go to the moment I tell you that will be the end of you in the present. You will also have no memory of how you got there except for knowledge of what is going to happen very soon in that moment. The third door, as you call it, is to accept being a member of the Time Patrol, to accept your past completely, and go through that door to your gate and on your mission. Do you understand?"

"I ken ye words."

"The day you killed the—"

"You think I regret that?"

"You wouldn't go to prison," Sin Fen said.

"I have no regrets over what I did that day," Angus said. "The only reason I'd chose to go back is to kill that bastard slower, with more pain."

The Metropolitan Museum of Art
New York, New York

Frasier normally wore aviator glasses to cover his orbital implant, but it was night and the Met was closed, so Fifth Avenue wasn't packed with pedestrians. Traffic rumbled by, but this late, the honks of irritated taxi drivers were notably absent.

At the edge of the street he raised his hand and a taxi pulled up. Frasier slid inside.

The driver waited for an address.

Frasier remained silent, until the driver turned.

"Where would you go?" the driver asked in a Pakistani accent. The man noted Frasier's solid black eye, but it was New York City and he'd seen stranger. But Frasier always wanted to be noticed.

"Cosmopolitan Hotel Tribeca," he said.

The Possibility Place

"What do you think of Angus?" Dane asked Sin Fen.

"He's solid." The two were standing on the edge of the Pit, looking down into the spiral of known history.

"What does that mean?"

"It means he's stable," Sin Fen said. "He's suffered terribly in his life, but he's made a sort of peace with it."

"Frasier doesn't think he's suitable," Dane said.

"Why?"

Dane turned to face her. "He thinks he's too old, too bitter, and his thinking is too narrow."

"Frasier's wrong," Sin Fen said. "He's old. He's bitter. But he's not a narrow thinker. I believe Angus will be a welcome addition to the team. I think the concerns there are a bit misplaced."

"How so?"

Sin Fen answered his question with a question. "How do you feel about Frasier?"

Dane considered that. "I've been snapping at him a lot. Irritated. I don't know why."

"Perhaps you sense something is off with him?" Sin Fen asked. "He hasn't been able to figure Lara out. That bothers him. He ignored your order to stay out of the team room, upsetting the delicate balance we must maintain with our Agents."

Dane looked back into the pit. "Lara heard a voice come out of the Pit. It warned her '*here there be monsters*.' Perhaps—" he stopped, considering what he was about to say. "Perhaps we should take that a bit more literally?"

"As in monsters among us?"

"Let's say problems among us," Dane said. "Frasier lied to me."

"About?"

"He said he had nothing further on Lara. Yet he's going to meet someone about her."

Sin Fen said nothing, knowing Dane and waiting for his decision.

"We'll have to keep a watch on him," Dane finally said.

The Missions Phase II

ZERO DAY; ZERO YEAR

"I told you," Ivar said. "I was just out for a walk."

"I have nothing to lose," Victor said. He nodded his head toward the body. "One dead or two dead, it's the same. The cleaners will take care of this." He shoved Fedex off the chair. The body hit the floor of the van with a thud.

"Have a seat," Victor invited.

As Ivar went past, Victor reached out and stopped him, doing an efficient pat down. He pulled the dagger and placed it on the console, then allowed Ivar to sit. The gun was in his lap, casually pointing at Ivar, who knew this man did nothing casual. He could see the barrel and it was pointed right at one of his eyes, although he couldn't tell if it was the left or the right, not that it mattered.

With his other hand, Victor drew the dagger. "Interesting. Our facility in the Negev was attacked by one man. All he had were two knives. Not the same as this but similar. He killed everyone there while infiltrating the facility. Heavily armed, well-trained men, with just knives. And he appeared like you. The security footage we recovered shows it. He moved very fast and the images are not consistent. There are times he simply disappears. Even on thermal.

"Since you appeared like him and are armed in a similar manner, please do not waste my time any more. How did you get here?"

"I can't tell you that."

"I should just kill you," Victor said, "since your group attacked my country and killed my comrades. I think—"

80

"That wasn't my group," Ivar said. "He wasn't from us."

"So there is an us. What group was he from, if not yours?"

"His name is Legion."

Victor nodded. "Yes. That was the name he called himself on the surveillance. Biblical in a way. Who are they?"

"Killers."

"Obviously. And you are not. I would have killed you in the park if you were like him, because you would have known I was coming up behind me and reacted. The only reason you're not dead is you didn't react. And I thought you might be the man I'm supposed to meet."

Ivar was relieved his lack of martial skills had saved his life. It was a small victory, but an important one.

"What country is this Legion from?"

Ivar didn't say anything.

Victor reached out and gently placed his free hand on top of Ivar's right forearm. Then he squeezed. Ivar screamed as incredible pain blasted along his nerves.

It is Now. Zero Day in Zero Year. How we got to be here via the computer timeline?

1970: A new company called Intel unveils the Intel 1103, with the first Dynamic Access Memory (DRAM) chip.

1971: The floppy disk, allowing information to be share between computers, is released.

1973: Ethernet is invented to connect multiple computers.

1974: The first personal computers are released, including the IBM5100, Radioshack TRS-80 and the Commodore PET.

1975: The Altair 8080 is introduced as the first minicomputer kit and two dudes named Paul Allen and Bill Gates write software for it and start their own company, Microsoft.

1976: On April's Fool, Steve Jobs and Steve Wozniak start Apple, introducing Apple I, the first single circuit board computer.

1977: Radioshack's TRS-80 sells out its 3000 copy first production run.

1977: Apple II.

1979: MicroPro International releases the first word processing program: Wordstar.

1981: IBM releases its first personal computer, Acorn, using MS-DOS.

1984: Macintosh.

1985: Windows.

1985: The first dot.com domain is registered, Symbolics.com.

1986: Compaq introduces the Deskpro 386.

1987: Only 200 domains have been registered in the past two years.

1988: The first major cyber-attack, the Morris worm, slows down computers to the point of being unusable—the inventor is convicted, and is currently a professor at MIT.

Victor let go. "The van is soundproof. I can make this a long night and in the end, I will get the information I require. You have no wallet, so you lied in the park. All you have is a dagger. You suddenly appear. You know of this Legion. What country are you from?"

Some things change; some don't.

"I'm American."

"You sound like one. CIA? Perhaps we are looking into the same thing?"

"How is that?" Ivar asked.

"If we are, you would know, would you not?" Victor reached out and Ivar flinched.

"Listen," Ivar said. "Something is going to happen in there." He indicated the displays of 60 Hudson Street. "Something I have to stop."

"Indeed," Victor said. "Why do you think I am here?"

The download gave Ivar a nugget. "You're from Unit 8200, aren't you?"

8200 was the Israeli Cyber Warfare Unit. It indicated the priority the Israelis placed on this new frontier of warfare that it was the largest unit in their army.

"No," Victor said. "They sit at desks and eat pizza, like my former friend here. He was just an expedient contractor. He will not be missed. But 8200 pointed us here. I am Sayeret Matkal."

The download informed Ivar that Sayeret Matkal was the Israeli equivalent of the U.S.'s Delta Force. Which reminded Ivar of—

Victor's hand shot forward, grabbing Ivar's shoulder and he applied pressure.

Ivar screamed and his body spasmed.

Victor's hand was gone just as quickly. "I need answers. What do you think is going to happen here tonight?"

"I don't know." Ivar rubbed his shoulder, the nerves jangled.

"You say you are American. What unit?"

"It's highly classified," Ivar said.

"Of course. We are friends, Israel and the United States. Some times. When our interests coincidence. But when they don't? We were recently contacted by the Americans about a possible link to the Negev incident. I thought you might be the contact. It's obvious you are not.

"Here is the thing. The man who attacked the Negev Facility, this Legion fellow. He infiltrated to rescue someone. A man, a boy actually, only sixteen or so, named Lukas. Do you know this Lukas?"

"No."

"What's even stranger is that this Lukas, he was a failed suicide bomber. He had a vest, but he failed to detonate. We learned, too late, it was on purpose. He wanted to be caught. He wanted to be taken to the Facility. He wanted to be interrogated. Rather brilliant actually. He knew our Unit 8200 was the best. It could find out information and he wanted information. And once he got it, his friend, Legion, came and got him out. Do you know any of this?"

"No."

"But you know Legion?"

"I know *of* Legion," Ivar corrected. "That's the name they all use."

"Yes. We are Legion. What country are they from?"

"I don't know."

Victor rubbed his chin, studying Ivar. "I don't want to hurt you but I will."

"There is an enemy," Ivar said, feeling his way. "An enemy to all of us. We call it the Shadow. Legion works for it."

"Shadow Brokers?" Victor nodded. "That would make sense. Unit 8200 is constantly battling them. We believe they are Russian, of course. But they might also be ultra-national. Similar to Anonymous. But they don't employ assassins."

Ivar noted that Victor would check the surveillance screens every few seconds. "What is the connection between that and you being here?" Ivar asked, not bothering to clarify that he didn't mean the Shadow Brokers.

Victor moved the closest mouse on the console and clicked on a file. An image appeared: Legion, on the street outside in daylight.

"This was picked up this morning; I should say yesterday morning. The same man who attacked our facility. He was doing a recon of 60 Hudson Street. That made us most curious. Which is why I was immediately sent here. That is who I want."

"I want to stop him too," Ivar said.

Victor nodded. "When Lukas and Legion had the information they wanted, they left the Facility. We later learned it appears they attacked one of your Black Sites. Also killing everyone."

"What Black Site?" Ivar realized asking that was a mistake as Victor's eyes narrowed.

"I do not think you are CIA or NSA. You are also a poor liar. And you are not trained well in covert operations. Who do you really work for?"

"I'm not at liberty to reveal that information," Ivar said.

"Would you die before revealing it?"

"I'd prefer not to do either."

A ghost of a smile touched Victor's lips. "You are a strange man."

"What were they looking for?" Ivar asked.

"They wanted the locationof a girl. It was strange. She had the exact same DNA as Lukas. Not even identical twins are a one hundred percent match. And 8200 tracked her down because the Americans were doing a search on *her* DNA, trying to learn who see was. It seems we both had a mystery on our hands. And everyone involved in it was killed in our Facility and your Black Site."

"Who was the girl?" Ivar asked.

Victor moved the mouse and brought up a picture of someone Ivar immediately recognized. "Lara Cole."

Zululand, Africa, 31 October 1828 A.D.

"They must all be killed, great King," Eagle said. "All the Grendels and the other, the Aglaeca as it is called. Before she gives birth. Then there will be thousands of them."

"You call me King," Shaka said, "but you are not of my people. Who do you serve?" Shaka picked up his *iklwa*, blood dripping from the steel blade.

"I serve all people, King."

"No one can serve all. One can only serve a single king. In my land, I am the All."

"Yes, King."

Shaka had the *iklwa* on his lap, ignoring the blood. And the moans and gasps of those still alive on the stakes all around the knoll. Eagle had no idea how many there were, but at least hundreds. It was recorded that after his mother died Shaka killed 7,000 of his own people for not showing enough grief, but no one really knew. There were no native records of events and those by the few Europeans after the facts were second-hand accounts. Stories told them, often by those with a desire to bend history to their own agenda.

The most pressing issues though, were where did the Naga *iklwa* come from, who had the old lady been, and how many Aglaeca were getting ready to spawn in the Valley of Death?

"You would already be dead if the witch had not prophesized your arrival and the arrival of the other."

Other? Eagle wondered.

"He came bearing a gift," Shaka held up the *iklwa*. He pointed the blade at Eagle. "Only this weapon worked on the beast you call Grendel. My warriors' *iklwa* could not penetrate."

"How did you get—" Eagle began, but Shaka wasn't listening. He was talking to the only audience he cared about: himself.

"I will kill you because you are not Zulu yet you dare pretend to be one. How soon that death will come and in what manner, will be—" Shaka fell silent as if he'd lost his train of thought. After a few moments he spoke. "I will burn you. You have scars from burning. So you will burn." Shaka smiled, revealing the two protruding teeth. "I have a man who is good at burning. Very slow." The smile faded. "But if you've survived burning before, then it be best to kill you another way. My mother would know."

"The beast, King," Eagle said, indicating the Grendel's head. "How did you kill such a mighty creature? That was a great feat!"

Shaka didn't seem interested in answering and turned as one of the impaled screamed. "They sound to me as if a young girl were singing to her lover. Yes, that is it. Death is my lover."

There was the rumble of thunder in the distance. The sky was overcast and the night warm.

"Who gave you that weapon, great King?" Eagle asked.

"No one questions me," Shaka said, but without energy. He slumped back in the throne. He looked down at the old woman in confusion. "Did you kill her?"

"No, King."

"She said two would come. She said there were beasts in the Valley of Death. One came with this gift." He indicated the *iklwa*. "I had him held prisoner until I saw the Valley of Death with my own eyes. To see if beasts were there as she said. They were." He lost his train of thoughts. "She had to die. She was a witch. But if she'd been a real witch, she would have saved my mother, wouldn't she have?"

Had the old woman been an Agent-In-Time? Eagle wondered. Or had she been from Pandora's timeline? Did it matter?

Eagle dismissed all those concerns. The mission was to destroy the Grendel and Aglaeca.

Shaka jumped to his feet, thrusting his *iklwa* into the sky. "You will not take me! I have paid the blood debt. Now you send beasts for me? You will not have me!" He turned to Eagle. "Will you fight with me?"

Eagle went to one knee and bowed his head. "Of course, King!"

"I fight also," a man with a strange accent shouted.

Eagle got to his feet.

A white man dressed in black leather breeches and tunic, carrying a spear and with a sword strapped to his side came out of the thicket of impaled. He walked up to Shaka and went to one knee, dipping his spear. "I fight the Grendel and Aglaeca with King Shaka. My life is to fight them and this is my last battle."

Salem Massachusetts, 31 October 1692 A.D.

"Enough of the BS," Lara said. "Why would Scout cease to exist? What's going to happen? What is that Legion up to?"

"It's here to stop you," Pandora said.

Lara gripped the haft of her dagger tightly. "I said enough BS. You just said it wasn't here for us."

"It's here to protect what the Shadow has already instigated," Pandora said. "Thus it will stop you from interfering if you try. Come with me. I'll show you."

Without waiting for her assent, Pandora headed toward the slightly downhill path.

86

Pandora spoke as Lara hurried to follow. "Since you seem to have some of the Sight, you should know that we are sisters. Did Scout tell you that?"

When Lara didn't say anything, Pandora continued. "We're part of a long line that goes back to Atlantis. We have been known as priestesses and oracles and sibyls and many other names throughout the ages. Even witches."

"Duh," Lara said.

"You are very similar to Scout," Pandora said. "But also different."

Lara wondered how Pandora could stay on the path in the pitch black under the trees. But even as she thought that, she could make out the trace of the lighter dirt among the bushes and grasses. Her eyes were adjusting and she could see into the forest on either side. Everything was lit with a soft green glow. There was a faint red glow to the left and Lara realized it was a deer, bedded down for the night under some bushes.

Deer weren't red.

But they were warm.

She looked forward. Pandora was glowing, red, with a blue halo flickering around the red.

"Far out," Lara murmured.

"What was that?"

"Nothing. Just thinking out loud."

"Thinking is good," Pandora said. "I hope you do more than just think."

"Stop," Lara said.

Pandora looked over her shoulder, but didn't halt. "What?"

Lara grabbed Pandora's shoulder and pulled her back. "I said, stop."

Pandora turned. "I don't have time for your games, girl. We—"

Lara pointed. "Look."

Pandora did as she asked. "What am I looking at?"

Lara sighed. "Can I borrow your spear?"

"It's a Naga staff."

"Yeah, can I borrow your spear?"

Pandora waited several seconds, then offered it.

Lara took the Naga and extended it forward, tripping the line across the trail. A log that had been precariously leaning against a tree thudded down.

"How did you know?" Pandora asked as Lara handed her staff back.

"I saw it."

"But I did not," Pandora whispered.

"That Legion dude wasn't out wandering in the woods twiddling his thumbs," Lara said. "You said he wasn't here for us, but he is here for us. He wants to stop us. Well, me. I don't know what your play in this is. So what *is* your play in this?"

Pandora was shaken out of her surprise. "The Shadow tried to eliminate your team on the last mission. But the Fates intervened. I knew your timeline was important, but I'm beginning to believe I might have underestimated that importance."

"You think?" Lara said.

"I thought your timeline would produce the One that is written of in the prophecies, but it might be something else."

"Yeah. Whatever. What is this One?"

"The One who will defeat the Shadow once and for all."

"That would be nice," Lara said. "A little more specific?"

"There is a legend that there will be one, of the line, a man, warrior, who will lead us to victory over the Shadow."

"Why does it have to be a man?" Lara asked. "Does the legend say warrior or man or both?"

Pandora was quiet for a few seconds.

"For real?" Lara was astounded. "Didn't occur to you a warrior could be a chick? Never seen *Wonder Woman*?"

"How far does your Sight go?" Pandora asked.

Lara pointed. "About that far. Enough to see the tripwire."

"Don't toy with me, girl," Pandora snapped. "This is not a game. This is life and death for entire timelines."

"I have no fraking clue how far my Sight goes," Lara said with heat in her voice. "I have no fraking clue about a lot of things. And I'm getting tired of word games with you. I can see why Scout calls you a pain in the ass. Why are *you* here? What's going on? Why is Scout threatened by what happens here, now?"

"Who exactly are you?" Pandora asked.

Lara literally growled. "You start answering. Or else."

Pandora was amused. "'Or else'? Don't threaten me girl."

But Lara was suddenly distracted. "It wasn't just Legion."

Pandora was confused. "What?"

Lara was looking at the dark forest that surrounded them. "The evil. There is more than Legion. This entire place is evil."

"Mass hysteria will do that," Pandora said. "Many of our kind have been the victims of witch hunts. Normal people fear what they do not understand."

"Yeah, yeah," Lara said, but she was still distracted. "It's more than the village. I can sense that up ahead. People. Scared. Angry. There are other things out here in the forest. Evil, no, not all evil." She paused, closing her eyes. "Death. Destruction. Hunger. It is all around us."

Pandora turned her head to and fro. "Be more specific, girl."

Lara opened her eyes. "The Shadow sent more than just Legion. Don't you sense them?"

"'Them'?"

"The monsters," Lara said. She shook her head. "Hallows Eve. Of course there will be monsters. I was warned and I told them. Here there be monsters."

"What kind of monsters?" Pandora asked.

Lara ignored the question. "Tell me about the Sight."

"Scout should have—"

Lara cut her off and there was something in her voice. "*You* tell me."

Pandora answered before she was aware she was answering. "There are four levels or stages to the Sight. First. Awareness of self. Second. Awareness of others. Third. Awareness of the world. And last, awareness beyond the world. I am in the Fourth level. Scout is floundering about in the Third. I don't know where you are."

"You couldn't see the tripwire," Lara said. "What good does the Fourth Level do you?"

"I became aware the Shadow was going to open a bubble in time here and now. I am aware that whatever change the Shadow wants to make in this bubble is in motion. I am aware that the Legion who is here has the task of maintaining the momentum of that which has already been done."

"And what has already been done?"

"A young girl is going to die this morning," Pandora said. "She is already on the way to death."

"What does that have to do with Scout?"

"It's Scout's great-great-great—" Pandora grew exasperated trying to number back ancestry. "Suffice it to say that she's a direct linear ancestor of Scout's. This girl dies, Scout never exists."

"Oh," Lara said. "Well, that isn't going to happen. Not today. Not ever."

New Delhi, India, 31 October 1984

"Your tea is getting cold, dear," Gandhi said.

Neeley gingerly picked up the cup and took a sip. "Who told you that you would die today?"

Gandhi waved a hand, dismissing the question. "Who is not important. I have always known I would die young. A hazard of my occupation."

The download had all of the team's previous missions. Other Agents had been met by someone who expected them, but they were usually either Agents-In-Time or killers from the Shadow. Scout had been met by Pandora on her Valentines Day mission. Neeley was mentally sorting through all 42 previous missions in the download for a similar situation, but Gandhi's words interrupted.

"If you are like the men I have in my intelligence units," Gandhi said, "you are evaluating this situation. Trying to understand. But you are not a man. Yet, you have a gun and know how to use it. But you say you are here to protect me. That is good. I do not want a woman to kill me." She smiled sadly. "India's first female Prime Minister assassinated by another woman? That would not sit well in history at all. So what are you to protect me from? There are many ways to die."

"I don't know, Prime Minister," Neeley lied.

Gandhi frowned. "You are American, correct?"

"Yes."

"Ah. I did not care for your Nixon, nor he for me. I feel comfortable believing history will not judge him well. But I find President Reagan charming. Not very bright, but he listens to others. That is a rare trait in a leader. His wife. She is the very smart one, but she has some strange beliefs. I suppose, though, that we all do. Are you CIA?"

"No, Prime Minister."

"I told you, Neeley, to call me Indira."

"Why do you believe you will die today?" Neeley asked, realizing that Reagan *was/is* President right now.

"I was always sick as a child so I have never viewed death as a distant thing," Gandhi said. She looked past Neeley at something, but Neeley kept her focus forward, not sensing a threat. "And I have many enemies. I had to reconcile myself to the possibility of an early death or else I would have spent every moment in fear and incapable of action."

"Why today?" Neeley pressed.

"I was told I would die some time this morning, after sun rise."

"Who told you this?"

"A vision," Gandhi said.

The download informed Neeley such visions were usually in the form of Valkyries. "An angel?"

"I do not believe in angels, dear. Although I could see how one would call it that."

"Why do you believe this vision?"

"I had one talk to me before," Gandhi said, returning her attention to Neeley. "And I ignored it. But it was true."

"When was this?"

"23 June 1980," Gandhi said. "Early that morning. I was told hours before it happened." She shook her head. "It warned me and I didn't listen."

The download supplied the rest: on that day, her eldest son, Sanjay, was killed in a plane crash while performing an acrobatic maneuver.

"You were told of your son's death before it happened?" Neeley asked.

"Yes. And I did nothing. I thought perhaps I was experiencing a delusion. A psychotic break. You see, after all, I am a rational person."

"Was it a being in white that floated in the air?" Neeley asked.

Gandhi nodded. "Yes."

"Did it tell you how you would die?" Neeley asked. "You asked if I were here to shoot you, so it must have given you some details."

"No. It was rather vague on that. The same with Sanjay. It didn't tell me his plane would crash. Just that he would die."

"But you acted like you were expecting me," Neeley pointed out. She looked around. "Where are your guards? Why weren't you surprised to find me suddenly here?"

"I was also told someone would appear here, very early, just after midnight." Gandhi picked up her tea. "Ah. It is cold." She gathered both cups and went over to the sink, putting them in and running the water. "Do you want more tea?" she asked over her shoulder as she turned the burner back on.

"No, thank you," Neeley said. "You do know your story makes as much sense as my suddenly appearing here."

"It told me someone would appear. Not an assassin. Someone to help me. I assume that is you." Gandhi clicked the burner off. She walked back to the table and sat down, sighing deeply as she settled into the chair.

"Everything I have done, I have done for the good of my people. However, I have not been a very good mother. My eldest died without the love he should have had over the years."

In the dim light reflected out of the kitchen, Gandhi looked older then her 67 years. The thick band of white above her right eye, almost a trademark, was the most striking feature. The rest of her hair, obviously died black, was ruffled and unkempt.

Neeley knew Gandhi had coerced her other son, Rajiv, into politics after the death of Sanjay. After her assassination later this morning, there would be reprisals against the Sikhs and at least three thousand would be killed. And of that carnage, Rajiv would simply say: *'When a big tree falls, the earth shakes.'*

Neeley was feeling less sympathetic toward Gandhi the more she accessed the download, much as she did on a Sanction once she read the file. Gandhi's 'poor mother' routine wasn't touching a maternal bone in Neeley.

Not that she had one.

Rajiv would also be assassinated in 1991. Which brought Neeley full circle. *Why was she here?*

Neeley picked up the .45.

Gandhi indicated the pistol. "You said you were not here to kill me."

Neeley glanced over her shoulder. A framed picture of a younger Gandhi with her family—husband and two sons was centered amidst a cluster of other pictures of the sons on the wall. "I'm not."

"Where do you come from?" Gandhi asked.

"I'm not from here," Neeley said.

"*When* do you come from?"

Neeley tried to act surprised. "What?"

"You come from the future, don't you? Tell me of it! How is death coming for me this morning?"

Neeley shook her head. "No idea."

"You're lying," Gandhi said. "I am a politician. We are liars and we know our ilk when we see it. You are not very good at lying. I suggest you never cheat on your man, if you ever have one. He will know right away. My husband used to cheat on me all the time. He thought he was so smart. He wasn't." Gandhi's voice had risen, but it suddenly switched back to normal. "Are you sure you would not like some more tea? Dawn is a few hours off."

Neeley got up and walked over to the wall.

The pictures had dust on the glass.

Gandhi walked over. "My family is—"

She didn't finish as Neeley spun about and pressed the muzzle of the pistol against her forehead, pushing so hard, the Prime Minister had to take a step back.

"You're delaying," Neeley said. "These pictures are part of a nice display you've set for me. You were told I was coming and I know what's going to happen."

Neeley took a step forward, the pressure of the muzzle causing Gandhi to take another step back. "I could kill you right now and end all this."

"But you won't," Gandhi said. "Because you were not sent to kill me. If you kill me it will change things, won't it?"

Neeley didn't respond.

"Look at your chest," Gandhi said.

Neeley looked down and saw two red dots flickering just below the hollow of her neck.

"Do you take me for a fool?" Gandhi shook her head. "I should have killed you immediately. But then I wouldn't know from where death come this morning? You would think of you were here to help me, you would tell me. But I don't think you are here to help *me*. The

93

vision simply said you were to help as vaguely as it said I would die. Death can come in many forms. It could be an assassin. It could be a bomb. I could have a heart attack. I could trip and fall. However, I do not think death is coming in a natural form. Because your arrival was not natural."

Doors opened and guards piled into the room. They were surrounded by a circle of men aiming their weapons at Neeley.

"Do you know whether or not you are in God's grace?" Neeley asked Gandhi, trying a Joan-of-Arc gambit as one of the guards took her gun.

Gandhi's eyes went wide. "*'If I am not, may God put me there; and if I am, may God so keep me. I should be the saddest creature in the world if I knew I were not in His grace'.*" She laughed. "A nice trap since one can't be certain of God's grace, but to say one is not in God's grace is to condemn oneself." Gandhi whispered so that only Neeley could hear. "Except I don't have a God. And you *are* going to tell me how I die before the sun comes up."

The North Atlantic, 31 October 1941 A.D.

The pressure on the blade against Roland's throat lessened the slightest bit.

"What do you know of Jagers?" the man asked.

"I know you hunt Grendels. And Aglaeca. Monsters. I've hunted with Jagers twice before."

"And you are still breathing," Jager said. "Impressive." He stiffened as the point of Roland's Naga dagger touched his side, just underneath his rib cage. "It took you long enough. I am surprised you survived two battles against Grendels with such slow reactions."

The rebuke didn't bother Roland because it was true. He *had* been slow.

Jager pulled his blade away from Roland, who returned the favor.

"You say this ship sinks?" Jager asked.

Roland nodded. "It will get torpedoed by a German U-Boat."

"The U-Boat is my target. This is not good. I thought this ship was designed to sink U-Boats?"

"It is," Roland said. "But the crew doesn't know there is a U-Boat nearby. How do *you* know there is?"

"I followed the doorway the Shadow opened. I saw where the beasts went. But I was too slow. I ended up on this ship. I was diverted by one of the Norn. Or she helped me. Who knows what those old bitches do?"

It took Roland several moment to find the term in the download: the Fates in Norse Mythology.

"She was there, just before the doorway closed. She also told me there would be a traveler in time where I was going. She was right about that, because here you are. You come from the future?"

First rule of Time Patrol. But Roland had been down this path before with Jagers. They came from another timeline, one that had been destroyed by an infestation of Aglaeca, who birthed Grendels, and Kraken, who guarded the nests where Aglaeca lay their eggs that birthed more Aglaeca and Grendels. It was a disaster that once it began reached criticality relatively quickly. And the Jager was saying that a Fate had already spilled the beans on time travel. Given that the previous two Jagers had proved to be formidable allies, Roland threw First Rule out the window. A move that would have surprised Frasier, but not Dane.

"I am," Roland said.

"And this ship is sunk by this U-Boat?"

"It is."

"Does it destroy the U-Boat in the process?"

"No."

They both staggered as the *Reuben James* took a large wave.

"That is not good," Jager understated.

"What is on the submarine?" Roland asked, although he had a pretty good idea.

Two crewmen came down the passageway, their foul weather gear soaked, their hoods low. They pushed past, not exchanging a greeting, exhausted after their watch.

"An Aglaeca," Jager said. "Many eggs. Some Grendels." He shook his head. "Something is not right. The Grendels would have killed almost all the humans on board. Just kept some alive to drive the boat. They would not risk attacking this ship. They would only fight for survival."

"What is their goal?" Roland asked.

"To plant as many nests as they can," Jager said. "Along coastlines. So the eggs can hatch and then the beasts can multiply until they over-run your world. As they did mine. Your timeline is at war?"

Roland nodded. "It is the beginning of what will be the largest war ever in our timeline."

"That would be a perfect time for the Aglaeca. That is why the Shadow choose now. Sow confusion amongst the fog of war. A strategy that has worked."

"So we have to sink this U-Boat?" Roland asked, wondering how that would factor into history, since the download indicated there was only one U-Boat in the attack and it survived. In fact, the U-552 would survive the entire war, a rarity. Unless, Roland realized, there wasn't going to be an attack since the submarine was infested with Grendels.

A lot of variables for Roland to process, with a lot of vagaries.

"They have to be stopped," Jager said, "or your timeline will be destroyed."

"Come," Roland said. "We must talk to the captain."

The download guided him along the passageway, and up a ladder, making the short distance through the destroyer to the bridge. The ship was a classic 'four-stack' *Clemson* class destroyer, built in 1919. This model was the most numerous destroyer class designed and built by the United States up to this point, with a total of 156 launched. It was a little over three hundred feet long by thirty-two feet wide. Its armament consisted of four, four-inch guns, one anti-aircraft gun, and some machine guns. The primary weapons for other surface ships were twelve torpedo tubes. For destroying submarines there were depth charge racks on the aft deck.

Roland led the way onto the bridge, Jager at his side. The captain and the others on duty turned in surprise at their unexpected entry.

"Captain Edwards," Roland said, the download supplying the name.

"What is it sailor?" The bridge was dimly lit as dawn was still an hour off and they were maintaining their night vision. Edwards squinted. "Who are you? I don't recognize either of you."

"Sir, may I have a word?" Roland asked.

Edwards had been next to the helmsman. He walked the few feet over to Roland and Jager. "Who the hell are you?"

"There's a U-Boat off the port bow." Roland looked at the large clock on the aft bulkhead of the bridge.

0532.

"In eighteen minutes," Roland said, "a torpedo will strike. The ship will sink."

"Hold on, hold on." Edwards held up a hand. "First. Who are you? How are you on my ship? How do you know about a U-Boat and torpedoes?"

"We don't have time for this," Jager said, his hand sliding inside his oilskin jacket for his dagger.

"Wait," Roland said to Jager. He stepped close to Edwards and spoke so only the captain could hear him. "You graduated the Naval Academy in 1926. You came in fourth in the light heavyweight division in freestyle wrestling at the 1928 Olympics. You've served on the battleship *Florida* and the destroyer *Reno*. You also have gone through submarine training. Your ship is going to become the first ship sunk by the Germans in the coming war, unless you take action. Immediate action."

Edwards wasn't impressed. "Sailor, tell me who you are or I will have both of you arrested."

An ensign in the bridge crew, picking up the captain's angry tone came closer, along with a seaman.

Roland could tell the Captain was exhausted. According to the download he'd been on the bridge almost continuously the last several days as the convoy approached U-Boat territory. In fact, the American escorts were supposed to have handed off the convoy to British warships the previous day, but there'd been a delay and the Americans had been asked to stay on one extra, fateful, day. The convoy was currently located seven hundred miles west and south of Iceland.

Roland continued. "You were born in San Saba, Texas on 9 November, 1905. And unless you listen to me, you're going to die today."

"You're crazy," Edwards said.

None of the bridge crew were armed, which Roland found odd, since he equated a soldier not being armed with being naked, but the Navy was the Navy and Roland had always found it to be a rather foreign branch of service. Roland figured it was time to pull their blades and force the issue.

He turned his head. "Jager, we must—"

"Captain!" A crewman wearing a headset called out. "We have a message from the Escort Commander. The *Tarbell* has picked up an unknown transmission and we've been ordered to run down the RDF bearing." He rattled off the numbers.

"Port bow," Edwards muttered. He raised his voice. "Helm, come about on that bearing. Increase speed to twenty-five knots. Sonar, start pinging for contact."

He turned back to Roland and grabbed his coat with both hands, pulling him close. "Talk! Who are you? How do you know all this?"

Roland was big, but Edwards had been an Olympian wrestler. The two were at an impasse for a few moments, then Roland gave in and took a shot. "I'm from NCIS."

"What?" Edwards was confused.

Edith's download, given she was a stickler for detail, informed Roland that NCIS hadn't been founded yet which meant his TV knowledge wasn't useful.

"Naval Intelligence," Roland tried.

Edwards was still confused. "But how did you get on board?"

Roland glanced at the clock.

0540.

Jager spoke for the first time. "The pinging. What is that?"

Roland answered what the download gave him: "Sound navigation and ranging. Sending out underwater pulses and get echoes back."

"No!" Jager cried out. "That will draw kraken."

"What?" Edwards was confused.

"We have a contact!" the sonar man announced. "Close, sir. Very close. Five hundred yards on this heading."

"Battle stations," Edwards yelled.

A klaxon reverberated through the ship and those off duty scrambled into their gear to rush to their fighting posts.

"Stay there," Edwards ordered Roland and Jager. He went to the command chair behind the helm. "Range to target?"

"Four hundred yards, sir!"

"XO," Edwards called to another officer on the left side of the bridge. "Prepare depth charges."

"Aye, aye, sir." The ship's executive officer relayed the order through his headset.

Roland was tense, the same feeling he remembered from being under mortar attack. Not knowing where the thing that kills you is coming from; he preferred to face death face-to-face. According to the download, the *Reuben James* was struck just past the bow by a single torpedo that detonated the forward magazine, blasting apart the front half of the ship, including the bridge where they were standing. No one survived from this part of the ship. He glanced at the clock.

0543

Seven minutes. At the rate the *Reuben James* was closing on the target, the destroyer should beat the clock. But Roland couldn't relax.

"Depth charges armed and ready," the executive officer relayed to Captain Edwards.

"Two hundred yards to contact. It's close to the surface, sir."

Edwards swung a large pair of binoculars up, trying to see ahead in the dark. "Anything from the lookouts?"

"Negative," the executive officer relayed.

"Standard dispersion on the charges," Edwards ordered, "and set for minimum depth. Increase to flank speed. We need to get the hell out of there before they go off."

"Aye, aye, sir." The XO relayed the orders.

"One hundred yards," the sonar man announced.

The hatch on the right side of the bridge swung open. A lookout stuck his head in. "Sir!"

"What is it?" Edwards turned to face him.

"There's something weird directly ahead on the surface. Some mass of, I don't know what."

"A submarine?"

"Uh, well, I don't know what it is."

Edwards brought his binoculars up. "What the—" he muttered.

"Fifty yards," the sonar man announced.

"Searchlights on!" Edwards yelled.

One of the bridge crew hit a switch and powerful searchlights bathed the bow and the sea directly ahead of the *Reuben James* in light.

"Oh, my God," Edwards muttered.

Roland and Jager pressed forward, ignored for the moment.

It didn't take binoculars to see what had caused the lookout and Edwards' reaction. The sea was writhing with a mass of what looked like massive snakes, but were actually tentacles. The bodies of the kraken were twenty to thirty feet long, their red, ropy tentacles two to three times that length.

"There's a sub out there," the XO called out. "Under those things."

"Hard port," Edwards ordered. "I want--

He didn't finish as the glass at the front of the bridge shattered inward and a tentacle shot through, the length covers in suckers, the tip an open mouth with sharp teeth, snapping, searching for a target. It found one as it darted forward, hitting the helmsman in the chest. The teeth crunched down on his rib cage and the kraken pulled.

The helmsman was snatched off the bridge.

Wittenberg, Germany, 31 October 1517 A.D.

Scout looked at the body for several moments. It crumbled in on itself, turning to dust, until there was nothing to indicate there had been a person.

She took a deep breath. Another. Walked to one of the pews and sat down. She remembered Nada had told her that you never got used to killing.

"This is not a game," she said out loud, as much to herself as the unknown woman.

Scout was startled when the old woman's voice was just to her left in the aisle since she hadn't heard her approach.

"No, it is not a game." The woman was dressed in a black robe and carried a rod in the crook of her elbow.

"Lachesis," Scout said.

"And you are the one called Scout, although that is not your true name."

"What's my true name?"

"Do not worry about the entity you just dispatched," Lachesis said.

"'Entity'? Was it his time? His fate?"

"His kind are outside of our purview," Lachesis said.

"What is his kind?"

Lachesis pulled back her hood, revealing thin gray hair and a face lined with age. Her eyes were pure white. "That is not for me to tell you."

"Of course not," Scout said. "Everyone has to keep their secrets."

"You have one or two," Lachesis said.

"Can you fill me in on them?" Scout asked.

"It bothers you to kill?" Lachesis asked.

"Of course."

"But it would have killed you. You had no choice."

"There's always a choice."

"Ah!" Lachesis tapped her rod on the top of the pew. "Do you truly believe that? Remember who you are speaking to."

Scout sat back, a little sick to the stomach. "You're as bad as Pandora. All questions, no answers. The riddles of the universe. Why did *you* interfere? He would have killed me the moment I arrived if you hadn't slowed time."

"Then there would have been no choice on your part," Lachesis said. "I wanted to see what you would do."

"And if he'd killed me in the 'fair fight'?" Scout was tired of the verbal sparring. She stood. "I've got things to do."

"Martin Luther is safe," Lachesis said. "You killed the entity sent to kill him."

"Not drinking your Kool-Aid," Scout said. "If my mission is over, why am I still here?"

"I wanted to have a chat. Another reason to keep it from ambushing you." Lachesis entered the pew and sat next to Scout. "My knees hurt when I stand too long, especially on a stone floor."

Scout automatically sat down.

"We registered what you did in Afghanistan," Lachesis said. "Very interesting. And then in Chicago."

"You sure Luther is safe?" Scout asked. "He posts the ninety-five things of his on the door this morning?"

"It already happened for you and your timeline," Lachesis said. "It is as it is."

Scout didn't have a response for that.

"And Lara," Lachesis said. "Very intriguing."

"What about Lara?" Scout asked.

"She succeeded, yet she failed."

"English, please," Scout said. "Succeeded at what and failed at what?"

"She helped you escape Chicago," Lachesis said, "but she couldn't go through the door."

"What door?"

"The door to her origins."

Scout sighed. "I don't even know why I ask."

Lachesis pointed at a coffer at the end of the pew. "*'As soon as the coin in the coffer rings, the soul from purgatory springs',*" she recited. "Quite cute. Simple. Simple appeals to most people. Simple answers to the complexities of life. It implies no consequences to actions if one has the means to pay their way out of the consequences. Quite naïve."

"Right," Scout said. "What do you want to chat about? The complexities of life? The vagaries of the variables?"

"In a manner of speaking," Lachesis said. "When you return from your missions, you see things outside of the tunnel of time, don't you?"

"Possibilities," Scout said. "What could have been if we'd failed in our missions."

"Why do you think they are only possibilities?" She didn't wait for an answer. "What if they are realities, other timelines, and the reason you see them is because out of the infinite number of possible timelines, they are the closest based on the event your mission went to and the branch points in an infinite multiverse?"

Scout considered that. "Okay. And?"

"How do you think the Shadow picks these bubbles?"

"Important events," Scout said.

"True. But, perhaps it only sees the closest timelines to the bubble point?"

"Why are you telling me this?"

"I want to show you some things. You want answers, now I will give you some." Lachesis reached over and placed her wrinkled hand on top of Scout's. The Fate's skin was cool. "Come with me."

Everything went dark.

The Possibility Palace

Moms was squeezing a ball, twenty times one hand, then switching it to the other. She had a thick book open in her lap, but her gaze was unfocused, her mind not on the page

The door to the room opened and Dane came in with Sin Fen besides him.

Sin Fen was a woman of mystery. Genetically she was a mixture of Oriental and European, an exotic beauty who turned heads wherever she went. Her age was impossible to guess; anywhere from an old thirties to a young sixties. Of more interest to Moms, and Dane, was her ability with the Sight. She was descended from the long line of Defenders who'd held fast on Atlantis until it was overwhelmed ten thousand years ago by the Shadow. She and Dane had some sort of relationship, the nature of which wasn't clear to any of the others. Sin Fen was rarely around and Moms suspected that she traveled to the Space Between, meeting with Amelia Earhart, and even further, most likely to other timelines to gather intelligence.

Moms acknowledged them with a nod.

"How are you feeling?" Dane asked.

Sin Fen knelt next to Moms' extended leg and put her hands lightly on the bandage.

"I'm breathing," Moms said.

"What are you reading?" Sin Fen asked.

Moms briefly lifted the book, exposing the title: *The Origin of Consciousness in the Breakdown of the Bicameral Mind*. "Eagle suggested it."

"An intriguing book," Dane said.

"Do you buy into his theories?" Moms asked.

Sin Fen nodded. "I think there's a lot of validity in it." She had her eyes closed, her hands going around the circumference of Moms' leg, and then she stood. "It is healing."

"Was Doc healing?" Moms asked. "You told him he was. He believed otherwise."

"Doc was done with this world," Sin Fen said. "Without the spirit, one cannot heal."

"Was he healing?"

"He was holding his own," Sin Fen said. "But his cells were damaged by his exposure in Pakistan. Some of them irreparably."

"I'm not getting a straight answer," Moms said.

"I can't give you one," Sin Fen said. "We did the best we could. There are things outside of our control."

"Like the Fates?" Moms asked.

Sin Fen nodded. "They played a large role in your last mission. If Lachesis determines that the measure of one's life has been fulfilled, then one cannot stop Atropos from cutting the thread of life."

"Who are they?" Moms asked.

"We don't know," Sin Fen said. "Perhaps the Ones Before. Perhaps they come from another timeline."

"So when our number is up, it's up?" Moms wasn't buying it. "No free will?"

"Doc had free will," Sin Fen said. "He made the choice that ended his life. Death is the most certain thing in everyone's life. In mythology, even the gods could not challenge the Fates."

"So the Fates are more powerful than gods?" Moms asked.

Sin Fen shook her head. "No. Think of them as acting parallel to gods."

"And who are the gods?" Moms asked. "We met the Fates. They're real. Are gods real? We've met Pandora, but she said she's not a god."

"She's not," Sin Fen confirmed. "She's human."

"Are there gods?" Moms asked.

"I don't know," Sin Fen said. She glanced over at Dane, then grabbed a chair. "You're asking questions that humans have been pondering ever since certain synapses made connections in our brains and we started wondering—is there something more? What are those bright things in the sky at night? Why does the sun come up every morning? Why? Why? And I know as much as you do. Seriously. I'm not hiding anything from you. Neither is Dane. We don't know who the Shadow is. Or the Fates. Or The Ones Before."

Sin Fen indicated the book. "Julian Jaynes says the gods were in our own brains when humans first started becoming conscious. Voices in our heads directing us. For example, he says that at the time of *Iliad*, those people fought because the gods in their heads directed them to, not because they chose to freely."

"Do *you* believe that?" Moms asked.

Sin Fen considered the question. "The *Iliad* is said to come from around the 8th Century BC. Atlantis was long before that and we were conscious then. Did we slide back after Atlantis was destroyed? Or were the people of Atlantis different from those outside of it? I suspect the latter. Our lineage—" she indicated herself, Dane and Moms—"is somewhat different. We all have a taste, more or less, of Atlantis genes in us."

"The Sight?"

"The Sight is part of it," Sin Fen said. "Our ancestors were the Oracles, the Seers, the people others came to for visions."

"And now?" Moms asked. "Do people have true consciousness?"

"It's one of the reasons we give you the Choice before you join the team," Sin Fen said. "Free will."

"Isn't that Choice pre-determined by everything we went through before?" Moms asked.

"You should concentrate on healing," Dane said.

"Lara heard a voice from the Pit," Moms said. "It said 'here there be monsters'. Any idea what that means?"

"The Shadow uses monsters," Sin Fen said. "Many human legends of monsters stem from real creatures that Shadow has fashioned. But I can tell you this: those monsters are real and are made using science. The Shadow is far more advanced in terms of manipulating gene codes. Kraken, Grendels, Yeti and the like are the result of splicing creatures that evolved naturally."

"Why don't the Fates just stop the Shadow?" Moms asked.

"I don't know," Sin Fen said. "But I'm working hard to find out."

"Work harder," Moms said. "Before we lose any more people."

Sin Fen stood. "Be careful of using the pills. They can cause problems."

New York City

"Cleopatra's Needle," Angus said. "I wager she was a wild lass."

Edith was surprised Angus recognized the obelisk, her personal touchstone for time in Central Park.

"There's one in London, ya know?"

"Yes."

Angus glanced at her. "And ya know the entire history, don't ya?"

"Yes."

"And you be aching to tell it to me." He held up a hand. "Spare me, please." He looked around darkened Central Park. "Isn't it supposed to be dangerous here? Death Wish and all that? Nefarious fellows lurking everywhere?"

"It's safe now," Edith said.

"Speaking of safe," Angus said, "do you trust that woman? Sin Fen?"

"I don't know her that well," Edith said. "But Dane trusts her."

"She lied to me," Angus said.

"About what?"

"About my Choice," Angus said.

Edith turned toward him. "What do you mean?"

Angus shrugged. "I don't know exactly, but I'm not some wee child to be told tales and I could tell she was telling me a tale. My Choice wasn't a choice, that's what I know. She read me and boxed me in to making the decision she wanted."

"I don't—" Edith began, but then her phone rang. She pulled it out and glanced at the screen. "We're heading downtown."

"Orders?"

"Orders."

"Let's be going then. Will we be taking the famed New York underground?"

"We'll take a taxi."

"Ah, just as terrifying."

The Missions Phase III

ZERO DAY; ZERO YEAR

Who the hell was Lara? Ivar wondered. How was she in the middle of all of this? Why was Legion after her even before she was with the Time Patrol?

Before he could mentally explore that murky path any further, Victor hit him in the chest, a quick jab, and Ivar doubled over, struggling to breath.

"It will take around forty-five seconds before your lungs will work properly," Victor said. "You will not die."

Ivar tried to gasp, but couldn't.

"I need to know who you are. Who you work for. Why you are here. In interrogation training they are very adamant that one should ask but a single question at a time. More than that confuses the subject. But I have been very patient with you, Mister Ivar. I need answers. You are hiding something very important from me."

Ivar finally was able to regain control of his diaphragm. He drew in a deep breath. "What year is it?"

For the first time, Victor showed some surprise. "Excuse me?"

"What year is it?"

Victor pointed at one of the surveillance displays. There was a time-date stamp in the upper right corner.

"Oh my God!" Ivar exclaimed as he read it. "We're in the present. Today is Zero Day. I didn't travel back." He tried to process this startling revelation. "That means nothing has happened yet."

"Ah," Victor said. "You are a time traveler?" He didn't seem surprised.

"What? Uh, no. I'm—" Ivar fumbled for what to say.

"Being a time traveler is one of the worst cover stories I have ever heard," Victor said. He reached out and grabbed Ivar's shoulder, the other one, and squeezed. This time he held it for several seconds.

Ivar writhed under his grip, until Victor finally let go.

"I want some truths," Victor said.

"You won't believe me," Ivar said.

"So you *are* going to try to say you are a time traveler?" Victor cocked his head. "It is a terrible cover story, so bad, in fact, that it holds the possibility of some truth. There are rumors. That the Russians and the Americans have meddled in things. But there are always rumors of strange things in our world. Of course, what happened in the Negev would have been dismissed as impossible except it happened. We have the video. I've seen it. So I know the impossible happened. But you say you did not travel back in time. Which means you are from now? This makes little sense."

"I don't understand it either," Ivar admitted, "but you have to believe me when I tell you I'm here to make sure our timeline is protected."

Victor grabbed Ivar's left elbow and squeezed.

"Frak!" Ivar screamed as Victor let go. "This bull is getting old. I lie, you hurt me. I tell you the truth, you hurt me. I got nowhere to go from that." Ivar closed his eyes, regrouping. "Entebbe. The Fourth of July. 1976."

Victor blinked. "Yes? What of it?"

"You say you are Sayeret Matkal," Ivar said. "So you know more about that day more than most, correct?"

"Perhaps."

The First Rule seemed out the window, which was getting to be a pattern on Ivar's missions. "I *am* with the Time Patrol," Ivar said. "We travel back in time to protect this timeline. Our history."

Victor didn't say anything.

"A team mate of mine went back to that day. To Entebbe. He parachuted in with Shayetet Thirteen. Into Lake Victoria."

Victor abruptly stood up and paced the few steps to the rear of the van, then back. "That can't be."

"Thirteen men," Ivar said. "They all died. Attacked by creatures from the Shadow."

"You're lying." But there was no power behind Victor's words. For the first time, he wasn't in charge of the situation.

"That part of the mission was never made public," Ivar said. "It's one of the most closely held secrets in Israel, isn't it?"

Victor stopped pacing. "Go on."

Ivar pushed ahead. "The Shadow is behind the attacks. The attack on your facility in the Negev. Not the Shadow Brokers, but another timeline we call the Shadow. Legion, assassins, work for it. I was sent here because we received intelligence there was going to be an attack on our timeline. Except it's always in the past. But this one was called Zero Day. Not a specific year. It's a term computer hackers use. We didn't know when it was, we just assumed it was in the past, because we always go back. It's supposed to be the same day, different years. 31 October. But today isn't 31 October. I don't understand it. Unless whatever happens now is somehow tied to 31 October."

"Do you go forward in time?" Victor asked.

"We can't. Whatever Legion has planned, we have to stop it. Do you know where Legion is?"

Victor indicated the monitors. "No. That is why I am here." He noted something on another screen. "Ah. We have company."

Looking at the screen, Ivar recognized Frasier standing underneath a street light on the sidewalk outside Duane Park.

Victor noted his reaction. "You know him?"

"He's from my unit," Ivar said.

"This Time Patrol?"

"Yes."

"Why is he here?"

"I don't know."

"If he is the person I am supposed to make contact with," Victor said, "it's about this girl, Lara Cole. And he is in the spot he's supposed be in." He shook his head. "Too much coming together at the same time. It cannot be coincidence. We have this Legion person in the area yesterday morning. This teammate of yours wanting to meet. And you arriving out of nothingness, thinking you've traveled in time, but you haven't."

"There is going to be an attack," Ivar said. "On the 9th floor of the Western Union building."

"To destroy our timeline?"

"To affect it at least."

Victor indicated the dead Fedex man. "I had him brief me on this place. It's a strategic hub, true. But if it's wiped out, the traffic will simply be re-routed to other hubs. There are others here in the city. 33 Thomas Street is more secure and the NSA uses it for Titanpointe surveillance."

Edith had included Thomas Street in the download. A 29-story building built to unique specifications. "Too hard to attack," Ivar said. "It's designed to withstand a nuclear blast. It has redundant systems so it can keep running for weeks even if everything around it is nonfunctional."

Victor glanced at the screen. "Perhaps your teammate has more information?"

"I don't think he knows I'm here," Ivar said. "He thinks I went into the past."

"We shall soon find out." Victor pulled out several zip ties and secured Ivar in the seat, cinching them tight around his wrists and ankles.

It is Now. Zero Day in Zero Year. How we got to be here via the computer timeline?

1990: A researcher at CERN develops HyperText Markup Language (HTML), leading to the rise of the World Wide Web.

1993: The Pentium Processor is introduced.

1996: Sergey Brin and Larry Page introduce the Google search engine.

1999: Wifi.

2001: Apple introduces OS X; Windows brings out Windows XP.

2003: The first 64 bit processor.

2004: Facebook.

2005: Youtube.

2006: NASA blocks all email with attachments for fear of being hacked before shuttle launches; plans for NASA latest space launch vehicles are hacked by some unknown entity.

Victor slipped out the back door of the van, leaving Ivar alone with the screens and dead body. He watched as Victor disappeared from view on one screen. Ivar shifted his attention to Frasier waiting outside Duane Park.

Victor appeared on screen, approaching Frasier. The two met. Ivar assumed they were exchanging the bona fides. Victor pointed back, toward the van. Frasier nodded.

Something flickered on another screen. Ivar looked, saw nothing for a moment, then saw movement. Fast movement through the park, coming up behind Frasier and Victor.

Ivar fought against his restraints. He screamed a warning, the sound trapped inside the insulated van. Victor and Frasier, despite their training and expertise, seemed oblivious to the danger.

At the last moment, Victor spun about, drawing his silenced pistol. Legion sliced his hand off before he could fire. With the dagger in his other hand, Legion blinded Frasier's human eye with a delicate slice across the surface.

Ivar knew of the Legion desire to make a fight last as long as possible, to draw as much blood from an opponent before the coup-de-grace. Knowing and seeing were two different things.

Victor, deprived of gun and hand, drew a knife from a sheath under his coat. He managed to block Legion's next blow.

Frasier had staggered backward several feet, hands over his eye. From what little he knew of Frasier's artificial implant, which could register temperature and other parameters, it wasn't quite the same as being able to clearly see. Thus as Legion shifted from his blocked strike at Victor, back to Frasier, his next strike neatly sliced off a layer of skin on the top of Frasier's forehead, a partial scalping. Blood poured forth, down Frasier's face.

Legion spun about, blocking Victor's thrust with one blade. With the other, he spitted Victor's knife hand by stabbing through the wrist.

Victor dropped the knife as Legion pulled his out.

Ivar could see Frasier's mouth wide open and he assumed the psychologist was screaming, but the van blocked noise from the outside as effectively.

The noise must have bothered Legion because he ended Frasier, slicing his throat.

Frasier dropped to his knees, both hands to his throat, futilely trying to stop the gush of blood. He collapsed forward.

Victor took several steps back. Ivar could see Legion's mouth moving, saying something. Victor shook his head, but stopped his retreat. Blood was pulsing from his severed wrist. His other hand was useless.

"Run," Ivar yelled, forgetting for the moment that not long ago Victor had been torturing him. "Run!"

Legion move fast, slamming a dagger into Victor's chest. The Israeli dropped to the pavement. Legion grabbed the back of his collar and dragged him to Frasier. Then he pulled both bodies into the park, semi-hiding them in the bushes.

Then, as Ivar had feared, he headed straight for the van.

Zululand, Africa, 31 October 1828 A.D.

"Your army awaits, King," the Jager said.

Eagle recognized his kind from Roland's debriefs.

"The last of your witch's prophecy is here," Jager said. "You can kill me as you have promised or we can kill the beasts sent for you. That is, of course, your decision as King. But we do not have much time."

"That is true," Eagle said. "Great King Shaka, we only have hours before it will be too late."

He had no idea if that was true or not, but he knew the bubble existed for a reason.

Shaka seemed confused. "Are you demons?"

Jager gave a slight bow. "I am but a servant, great King. As I told you when I first arrived, I am a hunter sent to help you against these beasts. They must die." He indicated the severed head. "It was a great feat of arms to have slain one. I hope the weapon I gifted you was useful in that regards?"

Shaka looked past Jager, into the darkness, above the bodies of the impaled. "You were right, *umama*. I am being tested." He shifted his gaze to Jager and then Eagle. "Come."

Without looking back, Shaka walked into the forest of impaled. Eagle and Jager hurried to follow.

"Where are you from?" Jager asked Eagle.

"Here."

"You lie. But it doesn't matter. We will both be dead soon. I have seen how he rules. I just hope he can fight as brutally."

A moan caused Eagle to glance up. A young boy was trying hard not to squirm on the stake. He was canted and the tip had come out of the right rib cage. His eyes were wide with pain.

"Sometimes I wonder who the real monsters are," Eagle said. He lifted the *iklwa* to end the boy's misery but Jager put an arm across his, blocking him.

"The King will take offense at your interference. The boy will be dead soon anyway. And I can tell you who the real monsters are. When the beasts over-run your world and feast on the bones of your children, you will know."

Eagle drew back the *iklwa*, trying to ignore the misery around him.

"Your spear," Eagle said.

"What about it?" Jager carried it in his right hand. The haft was wood, the tip of dull iron, a foot in length, going from a point to a four inch base.

"Does it have Naga steel at the core?"

Jager laughed. "You know of us."

"I know of you," Eagle confirmed.

"Have you fought with one of my brethren?"

Eagle considered the phrasing. Which held a couple of options. "One of my comrades fought at the side of your brethren. Twice. Both times they killed a Grendel and an Aglaeca."

"And the Jager?"

"Sacrificed themselves."

"And your comrade?"

"He survived," Eagle said.

"I always wonder about those who survive," Jager said. "Their side is the only tale we get to hear. I sometimes wish there was someone who could speak for the dead."

"The living speak for the dead," Eagle said.

"Only of what they know," Jager said. "The dead experience something none of us know. The knowledge will soon be ours."

At the base of the knoll, they were finally out of the impaled. Eagle and Jager came to an abrupt halt as he saw what awaited.

"Very good," Jager said. "They have been assembling all day."

Thousands of Zulu warriors were standing in formation. They were organized in *impi*, regiments of Zulus. There were individuals out front at regular intervals. As perfect as anything Eagle had seen during his time at West Point when the Corps lined up on the Plain for review.

Shaka continued walking as if there were no one there. Eagle and Jager hustled to keep up with him as he passed in the space between two *impi*. As soon as they were beyond the last rank, each group turned in perfect synchronicity. With a ripple of warriors, every *impi* shifted.

They began marching in the same direction, following their King.

The sound of their feet hitting the ground was a rumble Eagle could feel in his body and in his heart.

Salem Massachusetts, 31 October 1692 A.D.

The village of Salem lay ahead, a scattering of lights trying to hold back the darkness.

"No showers," Lara muttered.

"What was that?" Pandora said.

"Nothing," Lara said. She turned away from the village.

"We have to—" Pandora began, but Lara held up a hand, quieting her.

"Oh," Lara said. "He's a big one."

"Who—" Pandora said, but then snapped into a defensive position, Naga staff at the ready, as a tall, dark, hulking figure approached. Seven feet high, covered in dirty, matted, white fur, mouth opened, revealing long fangs. Much like a Grizzly, except more humanoid.

Lara knew what it was from the download. Moms had encountered its like on her Black Tuesday mission high in the Andes Mountains.

"Yeti," Lara whispered. She didn't draw her dagger. She raised her voice so the beast could hear her. "Yeti. Or is it Sasquatch? Bigfoot? Do you like that one?"

The monster halted at the edge of the trees, just ten feet from Lara and Pandora.

"I like Ts'emekwes," Lara said, surprised she could pronounce the Native American term correctly. She was staring directly into its eyes, which were deep set under a prominent brow and yellowish.

Lara held her hand up and took a step toward it.

"What are you doing, girl?" Pandora hissed. "It will tear you apart!"

"But you prefer Yeti," Lara said, the edge in her voice. "You like the high mountains. Not this place. It's too hot for you here. The air is too thick." She took another step forward.

Yeti cocked its head and emitted a low growl, but remained in place.

Lara continued walking slowly toward it. "You're kind of cute, in a big, teddy-bear-could-rip-you-to-shreds, kind of way. Easy. Easy, big fellow." She had one hand held up high. She reached him. "Come here."

Yeti bowed its head. Lara ran her hand through the fur with great difficulty. "You need a bath, but there's no hot showers here."

Yeti gave a guttural growl.

"You need a name," Lara said.

"Seriously?" Pandora said.

Yeti's head snapped up and the growl was louder and threatening.

"Hush," Lara said, to both Yeti and Pandora. "Who else is out there, buddy? I know there's more. And they're all not nice like you. You were just made bad. But you're not bad." She turned her head to address Pandora. "There's something else out there. Something cold. Something I won't be able to talk to. And Legion is still around."

"We have to go into the village," Pandora said. "We have to save Scout's ancestor."

Lara turned back to Yeti. "I'm gonna call you Buddy. Is that okay?" Lara continued. "You cover our backs here for a bit, okay?" She removed her hand from its head and went back to Pandora. "Let's go."

'Buddy' remained in the treeline as the two headed down the path into the village.

"What was that?" Pandora asked.

"You mean you can't do that with your level four Sight?" Lara said. "A little trick I learned in the loony bin. I call it edging. I learned it the hard way. You think Yeti is bad? Try a psychopath who cut someone up and stuffed them in a footlocker."

"What else is out there?" Pandora asked as they passed the first cabin.

"Bad stuff," Lara said.

"Vague much," Pandora said.

That elicited a chuckle from Lara. "You're learning. So what are we—" she came to a halt as they reached the village square. A gallows dominated the space. It was rudimentary: a cross beam held up by a tripod of thick logs on either end. The download dumped info about an ongoing debate about where the Salem witch executions had taken place, with 'Gallows Hill' being cited most often, but no one quite knew where that was. Apparently it wasn't a hill at all, but rather right here, in the center of the village.

For Lara one thing stood out. The beam was low.

"No drop," Lara said. "They strangled to death."

"They died," Pandora said. "But look there." She pointed.

To one side of the gallows was a pile of stones. Then Lara realized the stones were resting on a teenage girl's chest.

"She is one of us," Pandora said.

New Delhi, India, 31 October 1984

"I'll pull the trigger and end you now," Neeley said, her finger on the trigger.

"Your threat has no teeth," Gandhi said. "You kill me or whatever it is kills me. I am killed either way. But I do not think you will kill me or you would have already. I was told you are a guardian. That you have strict rules that control your behavior."

"I am a killer," Neeley said. "And I am not *your* guardian."

"I believe you." Gandhi smiled despite the muzzle of the gun on her forehead. "But you have not pulled the trigger."

Neeley lowered the gun, which was snatched from her hand.

"Put her in the chair," Gandhi ordered.

Neeley was grabbed by two men who slammed her down, tying her wrists to the arms of the chair. She noted that both wore the distinctive turbans of the Sikh. She checked their faces against the download, confirming they were the two bodyguards who were supposed to assassinate Gandhi later this morning. However, she could see nothing unusual in their demeanor at the moment other than focus on doing their jobs.

116

Gandhi was shaking her head. "I know that I will die in the service of my nation. It is my duty and my fate. Every drop of my blood will contribute to the growth of this nation and to make it strong and dynamic. But we have enemies."

With Neeley secure, the two Sikhs stepped back and joined the other bodyguards.

Neeley checked the download—this woman was essentially a dictator in a pretense of a democracy.

Gandhi sat down across from her. "We are reaching a critical stage." She put both hands on the table and leaned forward slightly. "We have enemies. Enemies within and enemies without. Those who reach great heights always have enemies.

"The Pakistanis think they can develop nuclear weapons? Never. They need to understand this. The snakes shall not rise out of the grass!" She thumped a fist on the table. "Are you really here to protect me? I don't think so. Why would I need such as you for protection? I rule India! I rule from the ocean in the south to the tallest peaks in the north. I ripped east Pakistan away and made Bangladesh." She stopped in her rant and stared at Neeley. "How could you just appear in my residence? That is what I want to know? I did not believe it could happen as I was told. But it is true. So the vision must be right about everything. Enemies everywhere!" Her voice rose once more. "You will tell how I am to die this morning!"

Neeley could see the two Sikhs finally react, exchanging a nervous glance.

Gandhi stood. "Since you choose not to speak cordially over tea, I will have to use other measures." She nodded at a rough looking man with sergeant's chevron's on his uniform sleeve. Neeley recognized the type: a thug.

This wasn't going to be subtle of good.

Edith Frobish's download tried to intrude with unpleasant data about various torture techniques used by the Indian police under Gandhi such as the Hyderabadi goli and—Neeley shut that down.

The sergeant gestured and two men rolled a cart up. He retrieved a full-head helmet and settled it over Neeley's head. She felt him stuffing towels along the bottom opening of it all around her neck.

She had a moment's wondering what the purpose was, but once more, Edith's download was unhappily helpful: to mute her screams.

Then the pain came.

117

The North Atlantic, 31 October 1941 A.D.

The *Reuben James* shuddered, slowing, as the ship's rear screws became entangled with kraken. Several of the creatures died, but their corpses caused the transmission to seize. In the engine room, the chief engineer reacted as he'd been trained, disengaging both engines from the shafts.

Roland drew his dagger, Jager at his side. The front part of the ship was covered with writhing tentacles, several kraken half out of the water, along the flush deck of the destroyer.

Another tentacle darted into the bridge and Jager leapt up, grabbing it just behind the 'mouth' and using his weight to slam it down onto a section of broken glass, severing it.

The sonar man screamed as a tentacle wrapped around him and he was pulled out, his scream fading and then abruptly ending.

"Full reverse!" Captain Edwards ordered.

"Engine room!" the XO screamed into the phone. "We need power."

Roland grabbed a fire ax, a better weapon for the current threat. He sliced a tentacle in half as it grasped for another victim. He turned to Edwards. "There's a sub under there. We have to sink it!"

The survivors on the bridge were in a state of shock.

Edwards looked at Roland with wide eyes. "What?"

A heavy machine gun chattered somewhere on the left side of the ship. A hatch at the rear opened and an officer, half-dressed stepped in.

"Captain, what the hell is going on?" he yelled.

A tentacle came up the ladder behind him, the teeth locked onto his lower leg, and he was gone.

"They're on board," Jager said to Roland.

"They can come out of the water?"

"For short periods to get victims, then go back under." Jager dodged a tentacle, leaving a long slice in it from his dagger. "We must get to the submarine."

The machine gun suddenly ceased firing. There were screams in the night. The remaining crew on the bridge were cowering in a corner, trying to avoid the tentacles. No one was at the helm. The *Reuben James* was at a dead halt.

"What is this?" Edwards demanded. "What are these things?"

"Kraken," Roland said.

Another machinegun was firing and tracers arced through the night into the sky, then swung down, into the writhing mass of tentacles covering the front half of the *Reuben James*. Roland estimated there were over twenty kraken assaulting the ship. Bullets tore into the creatures, but didn't cause them to back off.

Roland swung the axe straight at a tentacle darting toward Edwards. The blade smashed teeth and went a foot into the appendage, splitting it. But the kraken still managed to clamp down and wrench the axe from his grasp before pulling its tentacle out the window.

"We can not hold here!" Roland yelled to Jager.

"The submarine is in front," Jager said to Roland. "The beasts would not venture far from it. They are defending it."

"Oh, crap," Roland muttered as he saw a large form leap up onto the forward deck. "A Grendel just boarded the ship."

No more tentacles were lashing into the interior of the bridge.

Roland grabbed Edward's shoulder, trying to snap him out of his daze. "Can you drop your depth charges now?"

Edwards shook his head. "No. We'll blow ourselves up too."

The Grendel staggered as fifty caliber rounds smashed into it, knocking it overboard. Roland looked to the left, where two men at an anti-aircraft battery were manning the gun. They were snatched as a half-dozen kraken attacked their position. They were torn to pieces by so many tentacles simultaneously grabbing them.

No more guns were firing.

"They want it," Jager said.

"Want what?" Roland asked.

"The ship. That it why the kraken aren't attacking the bridge. We must withdraw.

"Then we have to hold the bridge," Roland argued. "We have to—" he wasn't certain what exactly they had to do any more. Several more Grendels were on the forecastle. The submarine was now on the surface, tentacles randomly draped on top of its hull, several Grendels on the deck. A larger beast, an Aglaeca, was in the conning tower. There was a pair of smaller figures next to it.

"They're intelligent?" Roland asked.

"Of course," Jager said. "We cannot hold here. We must withdraw and determine a way to destroy both vessels." He pulled on Roland. "Come."

Roland grabbed Edwards' arm. "Come with us, sir."

"My ship," Edwards said. "It's my ship."

"Forget them," Jager said to Roland. "They are being kept alive to operate this. We must go now!"

Roland glanced at the clock.

0552.

He followed as Jager cautiously entered the passageway behind the bridge. He led the way down a ladder to the center passageway but halted. A hulking figure was at the far end, silhouetted by the combat lights. Jager darted through an open hatch and gestured for Roland to follow. It was a small wardroom. As soon as Roland was inside, Jager dogged the hatch shut.

"We must be quiet," Jager said. "No loud noises."

"I thought they were just beasts," Roland said in a low voice.

"They can plan," Jager said. "The Aglaeca. Not the Grendels. If they were all just beasts, my people would have defeated them. The Shadow gave the Aglaeca enough intelligence and much cunning. They command the Grendels and kraken. And you saw next to the Aglaeca. Humans. Whether Legion or Spartan or others. That's the real leaders. They will split the Aglaeca and whatever eggs they already have between the submarine and this vessel. Double their deployment."

Several shots, then a scream echoed down the passageway outside.

"This isn't right," Roland said. "This ship should have been sunk by now. I've screwed up."

"This is worse than if they had just sunk the ship," Jager said. "We must destroy both."

"The depth charges," Roland said. "Edwards said if they went off, they'd sink the ship also."

"Where are these charges?" Jager asked.

Roland had the download but he'd also seen enough war movies. "The deck at the rear of the ship."

Something big was moving down the passageway, heavy footfalls thudding on metal decking.

Jager put a finger to his lips. The noise stopped as the beast, whether it was an Aglaeca or Grendel, paused outside the hatch. Roland and Jager drew their Naga daggers. Jager indicated he would go high and for Roland to go low.

The wheel turned, spun free. There was a pull on the hatch, but the interior dogs kept it sealed.

Roland and Jager waited, hardly breathing. Then the heavy steps continued down the passageway.

"It will be back," Jager whispered. "Had to be a Grendel. It will report back to an Aglaeca or the human in charge. It will know this hatch is sealed from the inside. That someone is inside. It will not let that pass. They are efficient and ruthless."

"Happy Halloween," Roland muttered. "It's two hundred feet back to the depth charges and then up on the deck. We'll be seen."

The wheel on the hatch moved. Someone trying to get in. A light rap on the steel. Roland glanced at Jager. Roland didn't wait for agreement. He un-dogged the hatch and edged it open. Captain Edwards, blood seeping down the side of his scalp, pushed past him and inside. Roland shut the hatch.

"They're everywhere," Edwards was babbling. "On the bridge. All over. Monsters. They're monsters." He grabbed Roland's oilskin coat. "What are they? What is this?"

Roland his hands over Edwards and spoke in a calm voice. "We have to sink this ship and the submarine. Kill all of them. It's more than just your ship. They want to kill everyone on the planet. Do you understand?"

Edwards was blinking hard, trying to comprehend, to process the unfathomable. He was a Naval Academy graduate, an Olympian, a ship's Captain. He'd passed through crucibles few men had ever experienced. He slowly nodded. "Sink both. Okay. How?" Before Roland or Jager could respond, he had the answer. "We detonate the depth charges."

"Wait," Jager said. "Will blowing up the rear of this ship destroy the submarine in front of it?"

Edwards considered that. "No. Even if we drop them, and they detonate underwater at minimum depth, they might be too far to insure we sink it."

"But it will sink this ship?" Roland asked.

"Yes," Edwards answered.

"One thing at a time," Roland said.

"If the Grendels are bringing eggs on board," Jager said, "then we can go the other way. Get in the submarine."

"One thing at a time," Roland repeated. He turned to Edwards. "How do we get to the fantail and the depth charges? There are Grendels—monsters—patrolling everywhere."

Edwards closed his eyes and took a deep breath. "All right. There's a way to get to the fantail and avoid that."

"Go," Roland said. "We'll follow."

Edwards opened the hatch, glanced outside, then gestured for them to follow. He led them to a ladder up, behind the bridge, to the top of it. Roland glanced forward.

The U-Boat was just off the port bow, a single searchlight illuminating the area between its conning and the bow of the destroyer. A gangplank extended from its deck to the low main deck of the *Reuben James*. A line of Grendels were coming out of a forward hatch of the sub, carrying bundles up the gangplank, onto the destroyer. Several others stood guard. The deck of the U-Boat was draped in kraken tentacles. Some of the creatures were on the surface, their pizza-sized eyes glaring up. With slightly more light, Roland could see one of the people on the bridge had a German captain's hat on. The other was dressed all in black.

Legion.

With the *Reuben James*' engines shut down, there were no lights on the destroyer. Outside of the bow, the ship was bathed in darkness. Edwards began climbing up a ladder on the forward mast to the crows nest. Jager followed, with Roland behind him.

They crowded inside the tiny space, seventy feet above the water. There was no sign of the lookout. Edwards leaned out of the opening and pointed further up, to the top of the mast. "The main antenna slopes down to the top of the after mast, just in front of aft four-incher. The main back stay cable slopes from there down to the fantail, right over the depth charges."

Roland couldn't see the or even see the top of the mast in the dark. "Will it hold us?"

"If we go one at a time, it should," Edwards said. He pulled off his oilskin jacket. "Wrap this over the wire and slide down."

"You go first," Roland said. "You *have* to destroy the ship. They're bringing eggs on board to breed thousands of those monsters."

Edwards shook his head. "I don't understand what's going on. This has to be a nightmare."

"It's a nightmare," Roland agreed. "But it's real. Trust me. Almeda will mourn but she will have a full and wonderful life."

Edwards was startled, significant amidst this catastrophe. "How do you know my wife? How do you know that?"

"Trust me," Roland said. "We have to do this. You can't let these things take your ship."

Edwards made the command decision. "I'll do it." He climbed out of the crows nest and disappeared into the darkness above.

"You next," Roland said to Jager.

But the Jager was looking forward, at the circle of light where Grendels were off-loading eggs onto the *Reuben James*.

"Will his wife have a good life?"

"I got no clue," Roland said. "But he went."

"Do you think he will sink his ship?" Jager asked.

"It's against his instinct to do so," Roland said, "but he will."

"How do you know?"

"I could see it in his eyes. He made the decision. He won't let them have his ship."

"A warrior," Jager said. "Yes. He will do it."

Roland climbed out, onto the top of the crows nest. Jager joined him.

Jager pointed forward. "Then we must do that."

"How do we get on board?" Roland asked. "We can't fight our way through the Grendels. Then there is at least one Aglaeca on top of the conning tower."

"Likely another inside," Jager said.

"And there's the Legion," Roland said. "How does a Jager fare against one of those?"

"They are deadly," Jager non-answered.

"Then how?" Roland asked. He had the schematics of the destroyer in the download. He could see the path that Edwards had gone on aft. There was a forward stay cable at the top of the mast to the bow, but then—

A bright flash ripped apart the darkness. The shock of the explosion shuddered through the *Reuben James*. Then a cluster of depth charges went off and the stern of the destroyer was incinerated. The ship shattered in half the front blasted upward.

The combination of the ship being destroyed and shock wave from the explosion hit Roland at the same moment.

No Longer Wittenberg, Germany, 31 October 1517 A.D. The Multiverse

"We're not in Kansas any more," Scout murmured.

Lachesis chuckled. "No. We're not. But that was an interesting story of possible timelines, wasn't it? One wonders how Mister Baum came up with it."

Scout glanced at Lachesis, suspecting the Fate might have a very good idea how the Wizard of Oz author came up with the story.

This was similar to the Return from a mission and floating in the tunnel of time, but it was different. Not just because Lachesis was at her side, but because she wasn't moving and she couldn't see any other timelines. Everything around them was the misty gray nothingness of—

An image appeared below. It took Scout a few moments before she recognized Washington DC. Rather the remnants of a devastated American capitol. The only clues were the stub of the Washington Monument and a fragment of the Capitol Dome. Where the White House had stood was flat glazed rock.

"A possibility?" Scout asked.

"A reality for the timeline you see," Lachesis said. "This is as it is."

"Why are you showing me this?" Scout asked.

The ruins faded to gray nothing.

Then the planet, far, far below them. So far below that Scout could see the edges of the planet curving away in all directions. But she was confused about what she was looking at. It was North America, but it was off. The eastern part of the United States was abbreviated. Florida was gone, just ocean blue. All the cities of the eastern seaboard were drowned. The Gulf of Mexico extended far inland, up the Mississippi and what had been the Gulf Coast was gone.

On the west coast, the Gulf of California extended up past where Los Angeles would be, except Los Angeles and San Diego were under water. The Central Valley of California was now a large bay, and San Francisco a cluster of islands.

"What—" Scout began, but the image shifted and she saw Asia, or what was left of Asia. Bangladesh was gone. The eastern part of China was inundated all the way to Beijing. Shanghai, Hong Kong, Qingdao were all gone. Most of South Vietnam was under water.

"This is the planet after both ice caps melt," Lachesis said.

"It's real?" Scout asked. "Or a possibility?"

"It is as it is."

"Did the Shadow do this?"

"They did it to themselves," Lachesis said. "They developed fast." Things were going grey as Scout noted that Australia had a vast inland sea. "Faster than your timeline. So they destroyed themselves faster."

"So you're giving me a lesson on climate change?" Scout asked. All was grey once more.

"No," Lachesis said. "There are many ways for a timeline to destroy itself. And then, of course, there is the Shadow."

"Why does the Shadow attack other timelines?"

"Because it destroyed its own," Lachesis said. "Not completely. But enough to be non-sustainable. So it rapes other timelines."

"It's not 'raping' ours," Scout said. "It's trying to destroy it."

"Yes."

"Why is it trying to destroy my timeline?" Scout asked.

Lachesis turned to Scout. "The universe is large. Beyond comprehension. Do you believe there must be other life out there?"

"Sure," Scout said.

"Why do you think Earth hasn't been contacted by other lifeforms?"

"They've seen our TV transmissions," Scout said, "and are steering clear."

Lachesis gave a thin smile. "Cute. But there is a theory that Earth has not been contacted by intelligent life because intelligent life never really reaches intelligence."

"What do you mean?" Scout asked.

"Truly intelligent life doesn't destroy itself."

The Mission Phase IV

ZERO DAY; ZERO YEAR

The back door of the van swung open and Legion entered. He wore black slacks, black turtleneck, and a black balaclava, leaving only his eyes exposed. He took in the body and Ivar zip-tied to the chair without apparent surprise.

"You are Time Patrol," he said.

It was not phrased as a question, but Ivar, who'd been in too many similar situations, decided to take it as one.

"No. I was—"

Legion sliced him along his left forearm.

"Frak!" Ivar screamed.

"Where is your HUB?" Legion asked as he sat next to Ivar and looked at the monitors.

"I don't know."

Legion's hand moved so far, Ivar could barely follow, but the thin trail of blood along his other forearm bore witness to the wound and the instant pain.

"It's blocked in my brain," Ivar yelled. "I couldn't tell you even if I wanted."

"So you *are* Time Patrol," Legion said.

It is Now. Zero Day in Zero Year. How we got here:

2006: MacBook Pro.

2007: Estonia government service computers are disrupted during a dispute with Russia over removal of a war memorial.

2007: iPhone

2007: The U.S. Secretary of Defense's email account is hacked by unknown foreigners.

2007: China claims Taiwanese and US hackers are stealing information.

2008: Databases of both the DNC and RNC in the US are hacked.

2008: Russian hackers attack Georgian networks.

2009: Israel claims Russian organized crime hackers paid for by Hamas, attacked its internet infrastructure.

Legion began typing on the keyboard, his fingers flying over it as fast as he worked a knife. Ivar tried to see what he was doing, but he couldn't see the screen clearly.

"I understand blocking memory," Legion said as he worked. "No pain can break that. But sometimes, pain serves another purpose."

Ivar knew he should keep quiet, but he couldn't help himself. "And that is?"

"For its own sake."

Legion's fingers paused and he cocked his head, looking at the screen. "This van is always within three blocks of the Western Union Building. It changes position every twelve hours and this city is so heavily populated, no one notices it. In a way, it is an Israeli spy outpost in broad sight."

Legion began typing again.

Since he seemed talkative, Ivar decided to engage him in conversation, remembering someone lecturing during training about gaining the empathy of a captor if ever in that unfortunate situation. It had not worked well with Meyer Lansky or the killers of the St Valentines Day Massacre, but there was always a first.

"What are you doing?"

"What years did your teammates deploy to?" Legion asked. "You do know that, don't you?"

"You know the years," Ivar said, "since your Shadow opened the time bubbles."

Legion spared him a glance. "A valid point. But I was offering a quid pro quo. You want information, you give information. Since you seem curious." He shrugged, his attention back on the screen. "You cannot give me the information I want, so I will have to kill you. You do understand that?"

"I'd prefer if you didn't," Ivar said.

"The Israelis trust no one," Legion said. He lifted his hands off the keyboard. "They invented Stuxnet in conjunction with the United

States. But in coordinating that malware, the United States revealed its own capabilities to the Israelis. A tenet of combat is that every offensive development leads to the development of a new defensive capability. And then a new counter-offensive." He pointed at the screen. "That is what I have brought up. A Zero Day vulnerability that has existed for years and has never been patched."

"Vulnerability in what?" Ivar asked.

"The NSA's own self-destruct," Legion said.

"Self-destruct of what?"

"All the NSA's programs," Legion said. "PRISM, MUSCULAR, all of them. Not exactly destruction in the proper sense. In fact, the opposite. Opening them up to everyone. Everyone can spy on everyone once this Zero Day exploit is released. Unit 8200 did an excellent job developing it. All data will be open worldwide. Nothing will be encrypted. It even has a subroutine to break down prime number locks that credit cards use for secure transactions. And we know one cannot count on the better natures of human behavior to keep them from using the information for personal gain. It will be chaos on a global scale."

Ivar was staggered by what that meant. All financial records, all utility controls, everything that touched the Internet could be touched by anyone on the Internet if this did as Legion said. It would mean the destruction of the world's computer infrastructure, which essentially meant the destruction of civilization.

"A doomsday weapon the Israelis have held for several years," Legion said. He typed for another few seconds then stopped. "Sitting here, in a van. In the middle of New York City. It is amazing how foolish people are." He glanced at a clock. "It will only take twenty minutes to completely upload into the servers in the building. Then it will transmit and spread. And there will be nothing to stop it." He hit a key. "It is uploading. This is as satisfying as the death from a hundred cuts. Not as bloody, but deeper and more devastating. It will cripple your timeline. It will--"

*****

"This the fellow?" Angus asked, tipping Frasier's head with the toe of his boot.

Edith blanched. "Yes. That's him."

128

"Know the other fellow?" He indicated Victor's body, partially hidden under bushes.

"No."

"Well, ye now know where your man went and what happened to him," Angus said. "But I assume we be wanting to know who caused the poor soul to depart this mortal coil? Looks like knife work. Bloody knife work. Why were we following him?"

"He was supposed to meet someone," Edith said, "but he lied to the Administrator about the meeting."

"He met someone all right." Angus was looking around. "Dawn's not far off. Whoever did this isn't too concerned about them being found. I imagine some poor soul walking his or her beloved pooch will stumble upon these poor fellows at first light. Give them something to talk about 'round the old water cooler later in the day." He became concerned as he saw the look on Edith's face. "You ever see a killed person before, miss?"

Edith shook her head.

"I apologize for my flippant attitude, then." Angus retrieved the gun from Victor's severed hand. "High Standard .22. A classic." He pointed at a Fedex van parked on Hudson Street. "Unless I'm mistaken, that don't belong here this time of the early morning. Shall we?"

*****

The back door of the van flew open and Angus stood there, Edith behind him. "How are ye, lad?" Angus asked.

Legion was out of his seat, dagger in hand, facing Angus. "They send an old man? Your blood will—"

Angus fired once, the bullet entering Legion's right eye.

Legion collapsed to the floor of the van.

"Only a fool brings a knife to a gun fight and then starts it by yapping instead of cutting," Angus said as he climbed into the van. He placed the muzzle over Legion's ear and fired again. "Gotta make sure."

But it was sure as Legion's body crumbled on itself, turning to dust.

"That be different," Angus said.

"Are you all right, Ivar?" Edith asked, as she tried to staunch the blood flowing from the cuts on Ivar's forearms.

Angus broke the zip ties.

Ivar ignored them both, jumping from the seat he'd been tied in to the one Legion had occupied. He saw the countdown.

19:47.

"It's too late," Ivar said. "The virus is uploading and we can't stop it!"

Zululand, Africa, 31 October 1828 A.D.

"Great King?" Jager said.

They'd been marching through the darkness for over an hour. The terrain was undulating, covering in brush and rocks, but little vegetation. The *impi* had shifted into long columns, following behind Shaka. They were on a six-foot wide trail, heading west. The march was a steady jog, what the army Eagle had been trained in would call *quick time*. The steady pace was eating up the miles.

Eagle was winded, but holding his own. The warriors behind him, and Shaka and Jager, were barely breathing hard. The download contained contradictory information about the ability of the Zulus to move quickly. Many modern historians debunked the stories of fast, overland movements of the large Zulu forces. Of course, they'd also been split on whether the Zulus wore leather-bottom sandals. Some claimed that Shaka had forbidden them, requiring his men to toughen their feet. On the opposite side were those who said Shaka made losing one's sandals a capital crime.

Eagle sided with the latter. Going barefoot was just dumb and while Shaka was obviously deranged, he was not stupid. There was also the fact that Edith had directed the support people to equip him with sandals. Edith Frobish did not get history wrong. The thought of her brought a smile to Eagle's lips, but he shifted his attention to Shaka as the King looked over at Jager.

"What is it?" Shaka replied.

"I can tell you the vulnerabilities of these monsters. Where your warrior's *iklwa* can do damage, King."

"Speak."

"The armpit allows one to wound it," Jager said, "but will not kill it. The roof of the mouth is fatal if driven into the brain. There is a weakness on the back of the head, at the base—" Jager indicated on his own head—"that kills outright. But one must angle the thrust exactly and with great force." He indicated with his spear.

All this was done as they continued their steady jog.

"The Grendels are killers," Jager continued. "They will guard the females, the Aglaeca, to the death. The Aglaeca like to lay their eggs in water, in places they dig out of the banks. All must be destroyed. Almost all that hatch will be Grendels, fighters, but a small percentage will be Aglaeca, able to produce more. They give birth at a very fast pace. They all grow fast. From birth to full size takes barely a week for a Grendel. Even the new born can fight immediately."

"What else?" Shaka demanded.

"Those are the important things, King," Jager said. "None must be left alive."

Shaka yelled and several Zulu officers came racing up. He relayed the information.

Jager moved over next to Eagle. "You are not Jager. You are not Zulu. You know of Naga steel and are armed with it. Who are you? Who was the old woman who prophesized our arrival?"

"Does it matter?" Eagle replied. "We have the same goal. Kill the beasts."

"It matters," Jager said, "if you are not of the here and now. This timeline."

"I am of this timeline."

"The now?"

Eagle didn't respond.

"How do I know you aren't from the Darkness?" Jager asked. "Sent to kill Shaka and stop his army?"

"Then he would already be dead," Eagle said as the download confirmed that the Jagers called the Shadow, the Darkness. "I would have never allowed him to issue orders to his warriors. How did you learn to speak Zulu?"

"I was given the gift," Jager said.

"By who?"

"She who sent me here. One of the *Norns*."

"A Fate?"

Jager shrugged. "There are three *Norns*. They determine our destiny. Not just that of men, but of the Gods also. They abandoned my timeline to the monsters and the Darkness. It appears they favor your timeline. No one can understand the ways of those beings."

"A *Norn* sent you here?"

"Yes. She told me what I would face. And that I needed the help of these warriors. She gave me the tongue to speak with them."

"Do you trust her?" Eagle asked.

"I am here. It is not a question of trust."

"What is it then?" They were heading into country that was more broken. There was the faintest hint of dawn behind them, a smudge of grey in the dark sky. Thunder still rumbled occasionally and Eagle could see flashes of lightning ahead.

"It is destiny," Jager said. "It cannot be changed. Even as we fought the Darkness, there were many who felt it was Ragnarok. And it was."

Edith *had not* added Norse mythology in the download for this mission and Eagle could give her a pass on that. He had some fleeting knowledge of it. Ragnarok was the Norse version of the Apocalypse.

"There is truth in all mythology," Eagle said.

"'Mythology'?" Jager spared Eagle a look of disdain. "It is everything. It is all truth."

Eagle noted that ridges were rising on either side and they were being channeled between them.

Shaka held up a hand and the long column of Zulus accordioned to a halt.

The Zulu King's top officers gathered tightly around him. Eagle and Jager were on the outside of the circle and couldn't hear the orders he was rapidly issuing.

The circle broke up, the officers running back to their *impi*. Shaka pointed his *iklwa* at Eagle and Jager.

"You come with me."

The columns were breaking apart. Some *impi* moving off into the darkness left and right, but the main group followed as Shaka advanced into the valley. The ridgelines came closer, until there was only about fifty feet of space between them. The storm ahead was increasing in intensity, lightning flashing every few seconds, thunder rumbling. The first patter of raindrops struck.

"The Grendel should be guarding this pass," Jager said. "Great King, how many did you see when you were here yestrday? How far into the valley did you go?"

"You question me?" Shaka didn't appear overly insulted. It seemed the prospect of imminent battle was returning some sanity. He pointed as they came upon dozens of bodies scattered on the ground. More accurately parts of bodies. Zulu warriors, torn to shreds. Most were missing pieces. "We met the beasts here last evening. These all died and I was only able to kill the one and then others were coming. At least ten. I withdrew. Because the witch had warned me of this place in her prophecy. I needed to see if it were true." He stopped and looked at the two. "And here you are. This pass opens up wider, in four hundred paces. There is a watering hole. Many animals go to it, but they go through here which is why it is the Valley of Death."

Jager was peering ahead. "The Grendel should defend in the same place. At the narrowest point."

"Perhaps they are busy with something else," Shaka said.

As he said that, the first screams came echoing back, bouncing off the cliffs on either side.

"The left horn," Shaka said.

Eagle looked up at the almost sheer ridgeline to the left. "They climbed that?"

Shaka turned away and signaled an advance, along with another hand signal. The main column began to advance. The first *impi* began to spread out, shoulder to shoulder across the valley floor.

Thunder mixed with screams provided the somber score. Eagle was to the left rear of Shaka while Jager to the right rear. Behind them were thousands of Zulu warriors. Eagle realized the second hand signal had been for a silent movement. Instead of stomping the ground in unison, the Zulus were sliding forward on their leather sandals, leading foot barely coming off the ground then being put down softly.

"What did he mean left horn?" Jager asked in a whisper.

"Shaka has drilled his army to fight like a bull," Eagle said. "Two horns. One on either flank. The bulk in the center." He glanced over his shoulder. "He might attack with this full force, or a token force to draw the Grendels forward. Then his full force, the loins, will sweep forward, while the horns come in from the flank. He sent his horns up over the ridges on either side. He ordered his left horn to attack first, to draw the Grendels to them."

"Ah," Jager said and that was all.

A cacophony of thunder shattered the air as multiple lightning strikes lit the sky. The rain came down in earnest, the heaven's unleashing a deluge.

The valley suddenly widened and the battlefield was upon them.

Eagle spotted at least a dozen Grendels ripping apart the much shorter Zulu warriors of the left horn. The diversion hadn't worked completely. A line of twenty Grendels was facing Shaka and his *impi* as they began to deploy at the mouth to the Valley of Death. Behind the monsters was a pool of water sixty feet across, half covered with reeds.

Shaka showed his leadership by charging ahead of his men toward the closest Grendel. Eagle was right behind him along with Jager. And over a thousand Zulu warriors were behind them.

The odds seemed with the attackers, but the reality was that the Grendels were genetically engineered killing machines. Twelve feet tall, covered in impenetrable overlapping green scales, they shredded the humans with four-inch claws. Their yellow eyes glowed with blood lust as they killed.

Shaka was jabbing at a Grendel with his Naga *iklwa*, trying to get inside the much longer reach of the beast. Jager and Eagle spread out, each attempting to get behind for a shot at the base of head.

The creature wasn't only big, it was fast. It smacked Shaka's *iklwa* to the side, then spun, the back of its hand coming at Eagle. He tried to duck, but the glancing blow sent him flying.

Eagle landed on his back, head ringing, body not immediately responding to his mental commands to get up, to get back into the fight. He lifted his head, seeing Zulus, blood spurting, flying through the air. Other trampled under, not only by Grendels, but by their fellow warriors, all anxious to get into the fight.

Piles of dead humans were growing around each monster. The left horn was almost completely wiped out, taking down only two of the dozen Grendels they faced.

In a flash of lightning, Eagle saw Shaka duck under a Grendel's grasp and drive his *iklwa* up, into the beast's armpit. Jager took advantage of that and slammed his spear into the base of the skull.

Eagle got to one knee as the Grendel crashed to the ground.

He took in the battlefront. Two more Grendels were down from the main assault, but Eagle sensed the rate of attrition was on the side of the beasts.

Then the right horn came charging from the right ridge, some of the warriors losing their footing and tumbling down. They almost made it to the watering hole, where the eggs were seeded, but two Aglaeca came roaring out of the slimy water, the last line of protection. They were bigger than the male Grendels, fifteen feet tall, with a ridge of black scales on the top of their heads, a foot high, sloping down along their back.

The two waded into the Zulus. Several of the Grendels facing the main assault peeled off and joined them, forming a wall around the hole.

Eagle realized the Shaka's surprise left horn initial assault wasn't what had drawn the Grendels back from the choke point. Something stronger than tactics.

It was time.

A small creature was crawling out of the watering hole. Three feet long, it was pulling itself out with inch long claws. It made it to firm ground and gingerly got to its feet.

The monsters were birthing and soon there would be thousands.

Salem Massachusetts, 31 October 1692 A.D.

"I am sorry," the girl whispered as Lara knelt next to her. "I was just trying to help."

The girl was on her back. Her arms and legs were stretched out akimbo, tied to stakes in the ground with cords. She was naked except for dirty pieces of cloth across her groin and breasts. Her hair had been roughly shorn, just stubble remaining. The stones were on a board that covered her chest and remained in place due to upright stakes on either side of her body.

There were fourteen stones on the boards, ranging in size from a couple fist-sized ones to the bottom-most slab, a foot wide by two long and three inches thick.

Lara reached out and began removing the stones.

"More stones," the girl repeated, her eyes closed, her lips dried and cracked. "Please. End it."

"Take it easy," Lara said. "We're here to help."

The girl's eyelids fluttered open, revealing bright blue eyes. She squinted, trying to see in the early morning light. "Who are you?"

"A friend," Lara said. The download was giving her all sorts of tidbits about 'pressing', aka *peine forte et dure*, as the French called it, which made it sound interesting, like everything that was said in French. It was pretty obvious what the ultimate objective was: death. Slow death.

"You gonna help?" Lara asked, looking up for Pandora.

"It is not my place to interfere," Pandora said.

"You're full of it," Lara said. "And you said she was one of us."

"She is of the lineage of Atlantis," Pandora said. "She has the blood. What her level of Sight is, I don't know."

Lara had all the stones off, except for the last slab. "It will be all right," she said to the girl. "I'm Lara."

The girl was breathing more deeply, although she winced every time she drew a breath. "I am Unity."

"Seriously? That's your name?" Lara asked as at the same time she lifted the last stone off.

Unity gasped as her chest fully expanded and she was able to freely breath.

"How long were you here?" Lara asked as she removed the board. Unity was nothing but a waif, weighing no more than seventy pounds and probably just beginning her teen years. Lara couldn't believe she'd survived this long with the weight upon her. She used her dagger to cut the cords to Unity's wrists and ankles.

"Today was the third day," Unity said. She grunted with pain as she gingerly sat up.

Lara took off her outer skirt and removed her cape. She helped Unity to her feet and put the clothes on her.

"What are you doing?" A man's voice called out. Three men, dressed in Puritan attire, came forward, one of them carrying a torch.

Out of the corner of her eye, Lara saw a dark circle appear behind Pandora. Who stepped back, into it, and it snapped shut.

"Thanks," Lara muttered. "Not."

"A witch!" the man with the torch exclaimed. "Did you see?" he asked the other two.

"She vanished," one of them said.

One of the men drew a sword. "Hold there," he ordered.

There were more voices and Lara and Unity were quickly surrounded by over fifty villagers, most of the men armed with swords or clubs.

"There was another here!" the man with the torch called out. "Another witch. She vanished! We three saw it with our own eyes."

"As opposed to someone else's eyes?" Lara said, but none of them heard her.

A man dressed in a black robe pushed through the mob. "It is illegal to interfere in a decreed punishment. She has not pled."

The crowd murmured an assent. A dangerous murmur that was strongly tinged with the anger of 'let's lynch someone'.

Lara could clearly see the rage, a bright red glow all around. "She can plead guilty or she can die?" Lara demanded. "What kind of justice is that?"

"Silence girl," Black Robe ordered. "Or you will suffer the same."

"I've suffered worse," Lara said. "You're all a bunch of crazies."

The closest man with a club raised it to strike, but Black Robe stopped him. "Hold, brother, hold."

The crowd was pushing forward. Unity was behind Lara, her hands on Lara's shoulders. "Protect me, please."

With the coming dawn, and the cluster of torches, Lara could see more of the crowd. "Seriously? Pitchforks?"

"By being released," Black Robe said, "you are implicitly admitting your guilt, Unity Hale. You have determined your fate and that is death. Immediate death by hanging." He pointed a long finger at Lara. "And you, stranger, by aiding her, show your guilt. You too shall hang."

The crowd approved, the way mobs do, with a roar of blood lust.

"Not today," Lara said. "I ain't hanging today. Hung. Whatever."

"Please," Unity whispered behind Scout. "Hanging will be fast."

Lara wasn't sure if the please was asking for help or asking her to let them be hanged, but it didn't matter.

"No drop," Lara said, not quite sure why that bothered her so much.

Someone, a woman called out dissent. "They must have a trial. It is only proper."

But that lone voice of reason was quickly drowned out.

Lara closed her eyes and focused her mind. The sound of the crowd abated. The tightness of the corset faded.

Buddy?

Lara distantly felt strange hands upon her body, grabbing, holding, shoving. She reached up and grasped Unity's hands on her shoulders, holding tight as the crowd tried to separate them.

Buddy!

A guttural roar from the edge of the village. The crowd went silent. Lara opened her eyes, seeing those closest around her, the ones trying to pull her and Unity toward the gallows, shifting their attention away.

Then screams as those on the outer edge of the crowd saw 'Buddy' stomping forward.

Don't hurt anyone, Buddy. Just scare them.

The crowd melted away, much faster than it had formed. By the time Buddy arrived, there was no one to be seen as doors were barred and window shutters slammed shut.

"Easy," Lara said to the Yeti. She turned around, shifting Unity's hands off her shoulders until they were in her own. "It's all right."

Unity was looking at Buddy. "He listens to you?"

"Yes."

"So you *are* a witch?" Unity frowned. "Oh. I see. He's sad." She stepped around Lara and put her hand on Buddy's chest. "Poor thing. What did they do to you?"

"Time to get out of here," Lara said. "I think the bad people will be back."

Unity shook her head. "What they did to him, I cannot fix."

"Yeah," Lara said.

Unity turned toward Lara and put her other hand on Lara's chest. Lara grasped it and felt a jolt of, well, something.

"You're troubled," Unity said. She was remarkably calm for someone who'd been slowly being killed for days, was freed, and had just met a Yeti.

"Trouble's my middle name," Lara said, wincing at her weak attempt at humor. "We've got to get out of here."

But then she saw something out of the corner of her eye. She turned her head. Bodies, dangling from the cross beam of the gallows.

Eight. Not just dangling but desperately kicking, squirming, hands tied behind back, ropes tight around neck, a bench that had held them lying on the ground.

Then they were gone.

"You saw them?" Unity asked.

Lara could only nod.

"That is what I saw last month. The last hanging."

Lara focused. "We have to go."

Unity pulled her hand back. "To where?"

"Right now, anywhere but here. Come on." Lara pulled Unity toward the path inland. Buddy followed. "Why were they doing that to you?"

"I heal people," Unity said.

"Like a doctor?"

"I lay hands on them and they heal."

"Oh." They reached the edge of the woods. "So you helped people and they decided to kill you?"

"It is not natural what I do."

"Duh," Lara said. She stopped, putting out her arm and halting Unity. "There are bad things ahead."

Dawn was far enough advanced that they could see thirty feet into the forest, but an early morning mist was draped over the ground. All was still. There was no noise from Salem behind them. No normal forest sounds ahead.

Lara picked up the dark emptiness of Legion coming toward them. And something else. Something cold, something with a primeval mind that she instinctively knew would not be conducive to edging.

The Legion came through the mist dressed in all black, a scarf covering everything but his eyes. At his side was a beast with the body of a lion, the head of a snake and the tail of a scorpion.

"Great," Lara muttered.

"Who is that?" Unity asked, finally showing a bit of emotion in her voice. "What is that?"

"The guy is Legion. The thing?" The download readily provided the answer since Moms had run into one in ancient Greece. "It's a chimera. Sort of. Usually they have a lion's head."

TMI, Edith, Lara thought.

Legion came to a halt ten feet away. He looked at Buddy. "What did you do to it?" The chimera was at his side, the snakehead turning to and fro.

"I said hi to him," Lara said. "Acted friendly-like. His name is Buddy. Say hi to him."

"Just speaking would not do this."

"Are you Joey?"

"I am Legion."

The chimera was sidling away from Legion, putting distance between them. Lara glanced at Buddy, wondering if it could take the monster, since snake head and scorpion tail seemed a potent combination. Of course, the first issue was whether Buddy would fight on her side. All she could pick up from the Yeti was a dull orange glow and she wasn't sure what that meant.

She also knew she couldn't edge Buddy and battle Legion at the same time. She put her hand on Unity's shoulder. "Can you—" she searched for the right word—"sense the beast?" She nodded toward the Yeti.

"If I touch him," Unity said, "I can."

"We need him to fight that chimera thing while I take care of Mister Legion."

"He's a bad man," Unity said.

Lara didn't think you needed the Sight to know that. "Can you get Buddy to fight with us?"

In reply, Unity went behind Buddy, reached up, grabbed a handful of fur, and climbed up his back, until she was on his shoulder. She leaned over, her head against his and began whispering something in his ear.

"I take that as a yes," Lara said.

Then, of course, she realized she actually had to battle a Legion, one on one, dagger to dagger, and she was completely unprepared for that.

Think ahead next time, Lara thought.

"I knew a Legion once," Lara said, the edge in her voice.

He laughed. "It might work on an ignorant beast but you wiles don't affect me."

"Just trying to make conversation." Lara noted that the chimera was curving around, focused on Buddy. And Unity. Which meant Scout. Down the line.

New Delhi, 31 October 1984 A.D.

The tips of Neeley's fingers were on fire from the narrow iron rods inserted under the nails and then pulled out. Her naked torso was painfully aware of over two-dozen cigarettes burns on the skin. Her mind had retreated from the pain, to an inner room Gant had taught her many years, utilizing Edith's download to feed her random information, almost overwhelming her consciousness. She was cognizant of what was being done to her. Felt it. But didn't allow herself to be drawn into it.

For now.

When the helmet was pulled off, it took several moments to come back to full consciousness. It was still dark outside. She was aware of the pain, of being half-naked, but most of all she saw the two Sikh bodyguards standing on the patio outside, nervously looking in.

Satwant Singh and Beant Singh.

"Leave," Gandhi said to the sergeant. She walked over as the man scurried out of the room.

"I am sorry," she said as she arrived at the small table. She glanced down at the cup in front of Neeley. "Your tea is cold." Gandhi pulled out the closest seat and slowly sat down. "It has been a long night. Dawn is not far off. My people have much more they can do to you, but there isn't time."

Neeley noted there was a lot of activity behind her, in the main room of the quarters. She could only get a glimpse but she recognized a sophisticated mobile communications center had been set up. Sophisticated for 1984.

"What are you doing, Prime Minister?" Neeley asked.

"What needs to be done," Gandhi said. "I have been thinking since the messenger came to me." She smiled. "I was not quite honest with you about the message. I was told I *might* die today. It was not a declarative statement but rather one of, shall we say, possibilities? I was told *if* it happened, it was punishment for my failure to lead my country into the future."

"You were lied to," Neeley said.

141

"The vision did not lie about Sanjay. It did not lie about you appearing. I will take what it said as truth. Now I need you to tell me the truth. You did not scream while being tortured. That is impressive. But you will scream. Eventually."

Time, Neeley thought. She had to hold out. Until 9:20 a.m.

That was hours off.

She doubted she could and because she doubted she could, she knew she couldn't. The pain would break through to that inner room in her brain and when it did, there would be nothing. Gant had told her early during their time together that everyone eventually broke under torture. Or they died first. He'd added that torture wasn't effective for interrogation because one couldn't trust the information that was relayed, but that didn't help the victim of the torture.

Neeley knew she would have to come up with some convincings lies.

Gandhi continued. "This has made me think. What would my legacy be if I died now? Have I truly failed my country? I believe I have accomplished a great deal, but yet the messenger came to me. Surely there must be something to that?"

Someone brought a tray with a pot over and carefully poured into Gandhi's cup, then Neeley's, as if she were free to drink it.

Gandhi took a sip. "Are you from the future? It would be marvelous to know what unfolds. What awaits my country. But I have always believed we make our own futures. We cannot rely on others. We must take control. So that is what I am doing.

"I had hoped you would be more upfront about where and when you came from. And why you are here. And what manner of death might await me. I had hoped, especially since you are a woman, that you were here to render assistance or perhaps provide guidance, but you have done neither. I must assume, then, that you are an enemy. Sent to stop me from my anointed task. That *you* are indeed an assassin and were just waiting for the appointed time after dawn."

Neeley was trying to follow the rambling words and disturbed logic, while also trying to keep away the pain.

"Therefore, I will solve the issue of my possible death and my legacy at the same time. I will allow you to see history, then you will die." She stood and leaned close so only Neeley could hear. "I am not a person to be pressured — by anybody or any nation. Now you will see what happens." She indicated the other room. "Karachi,

Hyderabad, and Islamabad will be destroyed by my missiles. Then my Army and Air Force will take control of Pakistan."

Neeley tried to process that. Karachi was the fourth most populated city in the world. Islamabad the capital of the country. Gandhi was going to do a decapitation, first strike.

But would the Chinese just to the north, and the Russians, on the same continent, react? And the Americans? Reagan was President. The man who'd joked about launching a first strike against Russia on a live mike; how would he react?

The others in the room, the generals and admirals, were quietly arguing, with many a worried glance at Gandhi.

"You can't do that," Neeley said.

"I certainly can and will," Gandhi said. "Your appearance was confirmation. We will launch exactly at dawn. The moment of launch is when you will be executed."

The North Atlantic, 31 October 1941 A.D.

Roland was airborne, hurtling through the air seventy feet above the dark Atlantic, toward a pool of light from the U-Boat searchlight. And a writhing mass of kraken tentacles and Grendels on the deck, scurrying back from the rapidly sinking *Reuben James*.

It was just like any other parachute operation, except he had no parachute. Time had slowed to a crawl, allowing Roland to notice things. Especially Jager just a few feet off to one side, also airborne.

They hit the ocean side by side, just missing the U-boat.

Roland sputtered to the surface, shaking his head to clear his eyes. The first thing he saw was the foot wide eye of a kraken staring back at him.

He introduced himself by slamming the point of the Naga dagger deep into eye. With his other hand, Roland anchored himself with a grip of kraken flesh and kept pushing the dagger, his hand into the eye, then his forearm, then his entire arm until the tip of the blade penetrated the creature's brain.

The eye went blank.

Roland extracted his arm, and blade.

"Let's go," Jager rasped, half on the body of the dead kraken just a few feet away. "While they are confused."

The two pulled themselves out of the water, onto the kraken's body, ran along it, and hopped onto the deck of the U-Boat. They were at the after end of the boat, all the confusion in the bow as the front of the *Reuben James*, lifted out of the water, looming above the U-Boat. The Aglaeca on the conning tower was bellowing something.

Jager had his dagger. "I will kill the Aglaeca. You kill the Legion."

An audacious and optimistic plan. Adding in the thick spider web of kraken tentacles wrapped around the conning tower, Roland didn't see the odds as being in their favor.

He grabbed Jager's shoulder, turning him around. "This way."

They hopped over a kraken tentacle, heading aft.

The U-Boat rocked in the water as the sinking destroyer brushed against the bow as it went under.

The *Reuben James* had gone down on the day history recorded, just not in the manner history recorded.

In the east, the first light of dawn was tinting the horizon.

Roland found the rear torpedo loading hatch.

A tentacle lashed by, blindly searching, barely missing Roland's head as he knelt down.

Roland turned the small wheel on the hatch as quickly as he could while Jager stood above him, dagger at the ready.

With a click, the hatch was unsealed revealing a pitch black, narrow, sloping tube.

Jager slashed as a tentacle came at him, neatly severing snapping mouth tip from the rest. It retreated but a half dozen more came out of the darkness.

Roland slid into the narrow, forty-five degree opening. "Come on!"

Hitting the end of the chute, Roland looked up. He could barely make out Jager's feet as he slid in. Then the Jager abruptly stopped. Roland reached up, grabbing his ankles and pulled. For a moment Jager was going in the wrong direction, out of the tube, then he abruptly came down on top of Roland, the hatch clanging shut above him.

"Seal it," Roland said, as he went to work on the inside hatch, using his feet to turn the wheel, a difficult process.

Jager didn't respond, but Roland heard him grunting with effort, trying to close the hatch.

The hatch at Roland's feet fell open and he allowed gravity to take him down. He fell to the floor of the aft torpedo room. It was dimly lit with flickering red, emergency lights. Roland rolled away, and got to his knees, dagger ready. Jager fell to the metal grate deck with a solid thud.

"Who are you?" Someone demanded in German.

A sailor faced Roland, large wrench raised.

"A friend," Roland said, pleased the German from the download came so easily.

He looked over at Jager and realized that the hunter's left arm was gone from just above the elbow. Jager was futilely trying to stop the blood pumping out of the severed brachial artery.

Roland dropped the dagger and wrapped both hands around Jager's wounded limb, squeezing tight, pushing his thumbs on the artery.

"Help," Roland snapped at the German.

The German whipped his belt off and looped it around, just above Roland's hands, the wrench handle underneath. He turned the wrench, tightening the belt down. Then he tied the heavy wrench in place, along the axis of the arm.

Roland let go, wiping his blood stained hands on his oilskin jacket with little effect.

"I was a bit too slow," Jager said.

The German turned to Roland. "Who are you?"

"Americans," Roland answered. "From the destroyer that just sank."

The man snorted in disgust. "The killer who leads the beasts didn't realize I was steering toward your ship until it was almost too late. Almost. I had hoped we'd be depth-charged and sunk. I heard charges go off, not far away, but not near enough. He went after me and I escaped here." He nodded toward the forward hatch. "I managed to seal ourselves in. But they still have my exec and a few others they spared. So." He extended a bloody hand. "Captain Erich Topp."

"Roland. And that is my friend, Jager."

"A hunter?" Topp frowned. "What is he speaking? Norwegian? Danish? He is not American."

"He's a friend," Roland said. "One who fights these beasts."

The deck shuddered.

"We are under way," Topp said. "My executive officer is doing their bidding. He has to or they will kill the rest of the crew. They already have killed most. Now, I don't care. They can kill us all."

"What is he saying?" Jager asked.

Roland held up his hand, his brain trying to sort out the different languages. A download could only do so much.

"What happened?" Roland asked Captain Topp. "How did they get on board?"

"Ah," Topp was disgusted. "Two nights ago. We rendezvoused with our supply ship, not knowing it had been infested with these things. And the sea around it was full of their *krake*. We were quickly overwhelmed although my men fought bravely."

"Where do they want to go?" Roland asked.

"Greenland," Topp said. "Do you know what these things are? And the man who commands them? He is crazy. He talks to the largest of the beasts in some tongue I have never heard. An animal."

"They're Grendels," Roland summarized. "The man is what we call a Legion. They are evil. They want to breed more Grendels and infest the world."

Topp was silent for several seconds. "It makes as much sense as anything else. Since none of this makes any sense. Beasts from legend attacking. The world has gone insane."

Roland didn't want to get into the entire time travel, Shadow, yada yada, rest of it. "Can we sink your submarine? Perhaps detonate your torpedoes?"

Topp indicated the racks on either side. They were all empty. "We had fired our full complement from the rear tubes. There are four left forward. That is why we were re-supplying. And the beast-man had us load those things that look like eggs. Hundreds of them. They are eggs, aren't they?"

Roland nodded. He looked over at Jager, whose face was taut with pain and pale from loss of blood. "The captain of the submarine," he said to Jager.

Jager nodded. "Can he help us sink it?"

"Working on it," Roland said. He turned back to Topp. "Can we disable the engines?"

"Engine room is the compartment ahead of us," Topp said. "There are Grendels there. The drive shaft is below us." He indicated the wrench holding the tourniquet. "I was trying to get to it even though I knew it is not possible outside of being in dry dock."

A distant, crumpling sound echoed through the hull of the U-Boat.

"What is that?" Roland asked.

"Your ship going to the depths," Topp said. "Its hull is collapsing whatever compartments still have air in them. It will sink faster and faster until it is in the darkness at the bottom of the ocean."

The sound diminished and there was only the sound of the U-Boats engines. But even that shifted.

"They are switching to batteries," Topp said. "We will be submerging."

The deck tilted, then steadied out.

"We are at cruising depth," Topp said.

"How deep is that?" Roland asked, uneasily eyeing the surrounding hull.

"We did not descend long," Topp said. "We are just below the surface. What ship were you on? I saw it briefly through the periscope. A *Clemson* class four-stacker. We were not supposed to sink an American vessel, but you gave many to the British. This is where the British should be escorting, not Americans. Your ship was in the wrong place."

"The *Reuben James*," Roland said, his mind on how to destroy the U-boat, ignoring the fact he was on board. It was one of his strengths in linear thinking.

Topp looked at Jager then Roland. "You are not sailors."

"We are not," Roland agreed without thinking.

"Who are you?" Topp asked. He spread his hands indicating all about them. "This is not, I don't even know what the word would be. You called those monsters Grendels. From the epic. And the *krake* are also mythical, legends to scare sailors. But these are very real. I have had some time to absorb it. Accept the reality of the unreal."

"This is an invasion," Roland said. He indicated Jager. "He is a hunter of these beasts. He goes where they go. I am—" he paused. "I am a traveler whose mission it is to make what is supposed to happen, does happen."

Topp considered that. "So what is supposed to happen?"

"These creatures, these eggs, must die," Roland said. He looked about the cramped compartment and accepted fate. "This war? This World War? It will kill many. But in the end, Germany will be defeated. Hitler will attack Russia. The United States will be attacked by Japan at Pearl Harbor and declare war not just on the Japanese but also Germany. Tens of millions will die in the next five years."

Topp's face showed no reaction. "Why should I believe you?"

"Do you know about the camps? The death camps?" The download was trying to intrude with dates and facts, but Roland blocked that.

Finally a flicker of emotion from Topp and for the first time he avoided Roland's eyes. "There are only stories."

"These monsters are also only stories," Roland said. "Over six million will be killed in Hitler's camps by your countrymen." He pointed down, allowing some facts to intrude. "U-Boats? You will suffer the worst casualties, percentage-wise, of the German forces. Seventy-five percent. Seven hundred and ninety-three boats will be sunk. Almost thirty thousand of your comrades will die."

"We don't have that many . . ." Topp began, but he fell silent. He sat back against an empty torpedo rack, his shoulders slumped.

Jager spoke. "What are you telling him?"

"The future," Roland said.

"Ah," Jager said. "He does not look pleased."

"He shouldn't be," Roland said.

"We have to sink this," Jager said. He shifted position, but it did nothing for the pain coming from the severed nerves in his arm. Blood was dripping from the limb, the clock of life winding down for him.

"I know," Roland agreed.

"We are dead," Topp finally said. "Perhaps we deserve it if what you say is true. At least for me."

Roland indicated the torpedo room. "What if we flood this compartment? Open the outside hatch on our way out?"

Topp considered that. "Not large enough. The boat will surface. They will blow out this compartment and continue on their way."

Jager lifted his arm and pointed forward. "What if we also open that hatch?"

Topp nodded. "Torpedo and engine room flooded? Yes, she will go down. But."

"But what?" Roland asked.

"We can't open that hatch until pressure in here has equalized," Topp said.

"What does that mean?" Roland asked.

"It means we can only open that hatch *after* we flood this compartment," Topp said. "We will be swept into the engine room. There will be no way out for us."

The Multiverse

"Look," Lachesis said.

At first Scout was uncertain what she was viewing. A large tree, many branches spreading out, and hanging from the branches— people.

At least two-dozen bodies dangled from ropes, their clothes torn from their bodies. They were dead. Their skin was marked from beatings, many limbs askew from being broken. Faces were bloody and shattered.

"What is this?" Scout asked.

"*Les Grandes Miseries de la guerre,*" Lachesis said. "The Great Miseries of War. There were drawings made of this. And other events of the Thirty Years War. The war begins a hundred years after Luther posts his theses. The action you were sent to insure occurs. The war starts between Catholics and Protestants, but like many wars, becomes much more complicated. Many countries and armies switched sides several times, which puts a lie to their theological justifications. Atropos would know the exact number, but around eight million died as a direct result of this war."

The tree faded as the view shifted, the ground dwindling below, until Scout could see the outline of Central Europe.

"It is odd that religion causes so many deaths," Lachesis said, "when the core principal is love."

"You got a point to showing me this?"

"Would you go back and change what Luther did in order to prevent this war?" Lachesis asked.

"No."

"Why not?"

"Our mission is to keep our timeline intact," Scout said.

"Even though you could prevent all these deaths?"

"The Shadow sent that Legion to kill Luther," Scout said. "And the Shadow wants to destroy our timeline. So the Shadow knows our timeline will be worse off if Luther dies."

"Logical, I suppose." Lachesis said.

Europe was gone and there was only gray.

"The beginning," Lachesis said as the grey faded and Scout saw a city set in the center of concentric islands far below.

A city unlike anything Scout had ever seen. A golden palace in the center, crowned by a magnificent golden tower rising almost a mile into the sky. There were other golden buildings around the tower on the center island. Then a ring of water, crossed in the cardinal directions by bridges. On the first ring were white buildings of various sizes. Another ring of water, another circular island. The buildings were not as nice, more industrial. On the next ring there were numerous fields and farm buildings.

Seven rings of land around the center island. Ships, similar to Atlantean one Scout had seen in the Space Between, were coming to and fro on the surrounding ocean.

"Atlantis," Scout said.

"Indeed," Lachesis said. "Well over ten thousand years in your past."

"This is my timeline?" Scout asked.

"This is every timeline," Lachesis said. "The origin. They are advanced, but not advanced. They are tapping into the power of the planet itself. But to try to control that which you do not understand is fraught with danger." She glanced at Scout. "Much like your present fools with powers that aren't completely understood." She reached out and placed her hand lightly on Scout's head. "They focused on developing their minds, which is ironic. They had the Sight. But they couldn't see." She pulled her hand back and pointed down. "They will soon tap into that which they cannot control. And there will be disaster. And out of that disaster will come the multiverse. Or, perhaps, the multiverse is already here?"

"You don't know?" Scout asked.

"I don't."

"I don't believe you," Scout said. "If you can show me this, you have great power. Clotho brought a boy back to life. It's said even the Gods bow to the Fates."

"Do you believe in Gods?" Lachesis asked.

"I don't even believe this," Scout said. "Why are you messing with me?"

"I'm sorry." Lachesis even sounded apologetic. "You wanted answers. I am trying to give you some." She indicated the tower. "That still exists in the Shadow's timeline. They destroy it in every timeline they get to. Because they know any timeline where Atlantis still exists is a threat to them."

"But you said they tapped into power they couldn't control," Scout said.

"The core of the planet," Lachesis said. "They tried to tap into it via a bore into the Nazca Plain, where the crust is thin. South America was devastated. Their mistake initiated the Ring of Fire, destroying the Pacific Rim. The mid-Atlantic Ridge gave way, but they were able to shield this center of their civilization. The climate changed."

"They destroyed Atlantis in my timeline?" Scout asked.

"Yes," Lachesis said. "Except it was harder for the Shadow to do in your timeline than normal. It took seven attacks."

"Same day, each year," Scout said. "What day?"

Lachesis shook her head. "It doesn't matter. What matters is those seven years gave the priestesses and warriors of Atlantis in your timeline something very valuable."

"That was?"

"Time. The most valuable asset of all. Time to learn. Time to plan. Time to disperse the bloodlines of the priestesses and warriors."

"My bloodline."

"Yes," Lachesis said.

"So how do we get to the Shadow and stop it?" Scout asked.

"Remember what I said about the development of intelligence?" Lachesis asked as Atlantis faded to grey.

"Yeah."

"The Shadow isn't any different. They've sown the seeds of their own destruction."

"They destroyed their world," Scout said, "but they—"

"I am talking about the present," Lachesis said.

"What did they do?" Scout asked. "What will destroy them?"

"You asked the correct question earlier," Lachesis said. "Why is the Shadow trying to destroy your timeline, rather than reaping it?"

"Answering a question with a question isn't an answer," Scout said. "You got that in common with Pandora. You speak in circles."

"There are some things that you can't tell someone," Lachesis said. "They must learn it on their own."

"Then why take me on this little tour?" Scout demanded.

"You said you would not change Martin Luther's posting," Lachesis said. "Would you change any of this?"

Images flashed by:

Ivar zip-tied to a chair inside a van, a body lying on the floor next to him.

Eagle, appearing dazed and confused, on his knees in the midst of a battle between Grendels and Zulus.

Lara facing a Legion, looking rather uncertain.

Neeley surrounded by men with guns.

Roland in the water, surrounded by kraken tentacles.

"Would you change anything?" Lachesis pressed.

"Are all those things happening now?" Scout demanded.

"Some are happening, some have happened. Some will happen."

"You're no fraking help," Scout said. "Will you send me to them?"

Lachesis held up one finger. "You can choose one."

"You're a bitch," Scout said. "Lara."

"So be it."

The Mission Phase V

ZERO DAY; ZERO YEAR

19:35

"Calm down, lad," Angus said, "and tell me what's ailing you so greatly?"

Ivar looked at Edith in confusion. "Who is this?"

"He's a new teammate," Edith said.

Ivar pointed at the screen. "The countdown. Legion uploaded an Israeli computer virus that will cause—" he paused, trying to figure out what exactly to say to explain such a complicated scenario—"our civilization to crash."

"Is that bad?" Angus asked. He didn't wait for an answer. "What's the timer?"

"The computer virus is uploading to the ninth floor of the Western Union building," Ivar said.

"Can you do anything?" Edith asked. "Stop it from here? Execute some sort of command?"

Ivar was already typing, trying to figure out what exactly was happening. "I doubt it. The software is encrypted and the program was developed by Unit 8200. They're the best. We're screwed. The virus is already in the system."

"You're talking software, right laddie?" Angus asked.

"Yes."

"But software needs hardware, din' it?"

153

"Yes, but—"

"Easy, lad," Angus said. "Ninth floor of what building?"

Ivar pointed at one of the monitors. "The old Western Union Building."

"You mean right outside?"

"Yes."

"Ninth floor?" Angus asked as he began opening lockers inside the van.

"Yes. What are you doing?" Ivar asked.

"If this is an Israeli vehicle," Angus said, pulling boxes off the shelves that lined the side opposite the consoles, "then it's rigged."

"'Rigged'?" Edith said.

"For destruct," Angus said. "Them fellows never do anything halfway." He dropped the floor and ripped aside a piece of the thick, sound-proofing carpet. "Ah, here we be." He hooked a finger through a metal ring and lifted a metal floorboard a tiny bit. Then he ran a finger along the lip of the floorboard. "Could be booby-trapped."

"What?" Edith was trying to keep up.

"Seems clean," Angus said.

"'Seems'?" Edith repeated.

Angus pulled the floorboard up and tossed it to the side, revealing several bricks of explosive connected with wires.

"A pretty boom this will make," Angus said. He frowned. "It's always the blue wire, methinks. Or is it the red?"

"Do you know—" Edith began, but Angus beat her to the punch by ripping all the wires out and holding up a fuse.

He pulled a shiv out of his waistband and slashed through the wire. He handed the wires and fuse to Edith, who instinctively took them. "We'll be needing that."

Then he scooped out the explosives, dumping them into a box. "You want to take this?" he asked Ivar. "Or do you want to get us in the building? I expect there might be a fellow or two trying to stop that?"

Ivar took the box.

"Edith, my dear," Angus said. "do you have a timer on your phone-thing?"

"Yes."

"Sync it with that timer, would you please?"

Angus kicked open the back door of the van and ran for 60 Hudson Street. Ivar and Edith hurried to follow.

It is Now. Zero Day in Zero Year. How we got to be here via the computer timeline?

2010: iPad.

2010: The "Iranian Cyber Army" disrupts the Chinese search engine Baidu.

2010: The US introduces Stuxnet to attack the Iranian nuclear program.

2011: Canada's government and National Defense face a major cyber attack.

2011: It's discovered that a worldwide cyber attack, dubbed 'Red October' has been operating since 2007, gathering data from embassies, military, energy, nuclear and other critical infrastructure systems.

2012: Facebook passes 1 billion users.

2015: Apple Watch.

2016: The United States Presidential Election.

"Anyone inside is innocent," Edith began.

"There are no innocents in this world, lass, except a new-born babe." Angus pulled open the door and hit the security guard who confronted them with an uppercut that lifted the poor man off his feet. He dropped to the floor unconscious.

"Stairs or elevator?" Angus mussed as he jogged through the lobby. He stopped at the elevator. "What floor was that now?"

As Ivar began to answer, he laughed. "Joking, lad, joking. I'm not that old."

Angus punched 9.

The elevator began to go up. Slowly.

Angus began humming *The Girl From Ipanema*.

"Seriously?" Ivar muttered.

"Second most recorded song in history," Angus said. "After *Yesterday* by some Brits."

"Really?" Edith asked.

"I'd never lie to you, pretty lady," Angus said. "Except if I have to," he added as the doors slid open and a security guard aimed a gun.

"Hold it right there!" the young man yelled.

"Sorry, not today," Angus said. He reached into the box Ivar held with both arms and extracted a block of explosive. "You shoot this, the entire place goes boom."

The guard's eyes widened.

"I suggest you be getting away," Angus said, stepping to the side and indicating the elevator. The guard hustled on board, his finger jabbing the close button.

"The younger generation," Angus groused as he surveyed the floor. "Ignorant."

Rows and rows of servers, as far as they could see, fading into dimness.

"Where are the maintenance people?" he asked Ivar.

"On call."

"Time, Edith?" Angus asked.

She checked her phone. "Ten minutes, twenty seconds."

Ivar nodded down toward the box he was holding. "Will this be enough?"

"Has to be, so will be," Angus murmured but he was walking forward, looking left and right, and up and down. He turned back to Edith, holding the wires and fuse, and Ivar, with the box of explosives. "Best you both put those down and leave me to the task. The elevator should be available."

"Angus, we have to help you," Edith said.

"Let me borrow your phone, if you might?"

Edith handed it to him. He glanced at the time.

10:00.

Angus reached out and cradled her face in both callused hands. "You already have helped, and it made an old man's heart beat quicker that such a pretty thing as you spent time with me, especially after where I've been, but both of you *get out now*," he ordered as he took the fuse and wires out of her hands.

He pushed both of them toward the elevator, shoving them on board.

When the doors swished shut, Angus turned to face all the servers. He put the fuse inside the box, picked it up, then began softly singing the *Colonel Bogey March*, which most would recognize done by whistle from *The Bridge on the River Kwai*.

Angus knew the words and as he got to work, he sang them:

"*Hitler*

"*Has only got one ball!*

"*Goering*

"*Has two but they are small.*

"*Himmler*

156

"Has something sim'lar
"But poor old Goebbels
"Has no balls
"At all."
Angus glanced at the phone.
8:00
7:59
"This is right fine mess," Angus muttered.

Zululand, Africa, 31 October 1828 A.D.

Eagle staggered to his feet. He distantly noted that Shaka and Jager had taken down another Grendel and were on to a third. An efficient human killing machine. Perhaps they could turn the tide.

But it would be too late.

A bolt of lightning hit the ridgeline to the left with a thunderous clap and the sound of rock splintering. It was as if the planet itself were rebelling against this unnatural assault on the timeline.

A Zulu warrior had managed to break through the line of Grendels and Aglaeca and went straight for the newborn Grendel.

He died, stunned at the speed with which the newborn beast ducked under his *iklwa* and gutted him. They were not going to be babes for the taking.

And when there were more?

A second Grendel crawled out of the reeds.

The rain was washing a river of blood into the mud. Lightning helped the growing dawn illuminate the surreal battle.

Over two-thirds of the Zulu army was dead. Half the defending Grendels had been taken down. Both Aglaeca were still battling.

Eagle gathered himself. He sprinted toward Jager and Shaka who were taking on another Grendel.

Just before Eagle got to them, Shaka slipped in bloody mud and the Grendel slammed a hand, claws extended, into the Zulu King's abdomen. The tips of the claws came out Shaka's back as the Grendel lifted him into the air.

Jager used the moment to shove his spear into the base of the monster's skull. It collapsed to its knees, with Shaka still in its grasp.

The Zulu King struck with his *iklwa* into its mouth, driving with all his might, using the claws in his body as leverage, the tip of the blade going into the brain.

The Grendel collapsed forward, onto Shaka Zulu, killing the King.

"Give me your spear," Eagle yelled to Jager, striving to be heard above the screams and thunder.

"What?" Jager was momentarily confused, pulling his spear out of the corpse.

Eagle tossed his Naga *iklwa* to Jager, who automatically caught it with his free hand.

"Give me the spear!" Eagle ordered.

Jager tested the balance of the *iklwa* and tossed his spear to Eagle. Jager turned and charged the next Grendel.

Eagle jumped over the body of the Grendel lying on top of Shaka Zulu and raced toward the water hole. A third 'baby' Grendel was crawling out of the water. Eagle dodged it, splashing into the water until he was waist deep. He felt something slither past his legs, but ignored it.

He knelt, the water to his chin. He held the spear up, the base of the iron blade in the water, the tip toward the sky. "Please!" he whispered.

A face poked out of the water, peering at him. A 'baby' Grendel. It's mouth opened, reveling teeth already big enough to rip Eagle's throat out.

That's when the bolt of lightning hit the tip of the spear, soared through it, and Eagle, and into the water.

Salem Massachusetts, 31 October 1692 A.D.

"What do you say we try some trivia?" Lara suggested. "Or rock, paper, scissors?"

Legion laughed. "You're going to die." He spun the knife in his hand, faster than Lara could track. "Slowly and painfully."

"Show-off," Lara said.

"You are a bad man," Unity said, in a surprisingly clear voice. She whispered something in Buddy's ear and the Yeti stomped forward toward the chimera.

"Might want to—" Lara began but fell silent.

Both she and Legion watched as the two beasts, Unity clinging on for her life, battled.

Chimera struck the first blow, feinting with snakehead while the scorpion tail embedded itself in Buddy's right thigh.

That appeared a Pyrrhic victory as Buddy reached down and seized the tail with both hands. Buddy roared as he ripped the tail apart.

Chimera hissed and backed up several steps, the stub of its tail waving about wildly.

"That's gotta hurt," Lara said.

Buddy charged. The snakehead struck forward, but Buddy was faster, grabbing it. In not the safest way possible, one hand disappearing into the chimera's wide open mouth, the other grabbing the neck.

Chimera bit down, fangs sinking deep into Buddy's forearm. Which was exactly what Buddy wanted as it twisted its massive arm while keeping a tight grip on the neck.

The sound of the monster's neck breaking was very clear.

Chimera dropped like a stone. After a few seconds, the carcass crumbled inward, leaving no trace.

Buddy dropped to his knees with a thud, poison from both scorpion and snake coursing through his system.

"No!" Unity yelled. She let go of his fur and slid off. She scurried around to the front of the Yeti. She put both hands on its chest. "Stay with me."

Buddy whined, leaning his head forward, brushing against the top of Unity's head.

Lara felt her chest seize, feeling Unity's pain. She gasped for breath as Buddy crumbled to black dust and was gone, Unity's hands coming together, touching nothing between.

Unity went to her knees, running her fingers through the recently fallen leaves. "Oh, you poor thing."

Lara looked at Legion. "Let's finish it."

Everything went black for a second, and then Lara wasn't in the forest any more.

I'm in the kitchen. The one I don't want to be in.

A man stands there. Joey. Blood dripping from a blade in his hand. The blood trail leads through that door. The one I can't go through.

But I am not alone. I know it through everything that is me, every cell of my being. That is more than me.

Nada's voice is so clear. How the frak do I know it's Nada? Never met the dude.

'Here there be a monster'

I focus on the monster.

Joey.

Legion.

The face of the Shadow.

Joey looks about and shakes his head. "Nice trick. No wonder they were killing you witches there. But you can die here just as easily."

"I don't think so. I'm not alone."

"You said that before. Then you ran away. Are you Lara? Or Lily? Who are you?" *He smiles, but it's one of those smiles, you know, nothing nice at all about it. He lifts the blade.* "You want some pie?"

Funny guy he isn't.

"I didn't kill my family."

Joey shrugs. "So?"

"I'm not sure I come from a family." *Where did that originate?*

Joey frowns. "Let me end your miserable existence."

"I kind of like my miserable existence." *I walk toward him. It's surprisingly easy after all the struggles I've had in this room.*

Joey takes two steps back in surprise, then assumes a fighting stance. I stop, trying to remember some of the things they taught me. As if that's going to help me take this guy?

But then his eyes widen, darting to my right. He takes another step back, toward the door.

There's someone else here. Really here. On my right—Scout. Not quite real but not unreal either. Yeah, I know that don't make sense, but something flickers in his eyes. He can see her too. So maybe actually here?

And he's scared.

"You can run," *I tell him, trying to sound magnanimous. Where the frak did that word come from?*

"We don't retreat."

"You already have," *I says to him. The problem I got is whether Scout is real or just an image? If she's real, I think we can take this jerk together. But if she's not real?*

"Scout?"

"Yes?" That's a voice. A real one. I think. But given my past, I've heard a lot of voices I thought were real.

"You really there?"

"Yep."

Joes takes another step back, but he's got nowhere else to go, unless he retreats through that door.

Which he does.

"Let's get him," Scout says just as I knew that was she was gonna say.

"I don't—" "I begin but Scout doesn't let me.

"In every generation there is a chosen one... she alone will stand against the vampires, the demons and the forces of darkness. She is the slayer'."

"I'm not Buffy," I mutter, but I know it doesn't matter now. "Come on."

I stride forward, Buffy style, and shove the door open.

It's not the living room. There's no murdered family.

It's a Gate and before I can stop, even as I try to stop, I'm in it and through.

I panic. Did she follow?

But Scout is there. My 'Scooby' gang.

Joey is fifteen feet away, facing us, daggers ready, looking none-too-happy.

We're in a building, dark interior. Warehouse. Something big dimly lit with tall, narrow windows on the side, full of crap. It's cold, very cold.

There are containers in neat rows all about. Not containers. Black pods. Rows and rows; except for two nearby, which are separate from the rest and red, not black.

"Uh, Lara?"

"Yeah, Scout?" I'm trying to figure out how the two of us can take Joey, because the way he's standing, he ain't backing up any more. He has that stance, that crazy look in his eye, the look I used to see on the Fourth Floor of the loony bin. From the worst of the loons, the ones who chop you up and—

"Lara?"

I glance at Scout, keeping tabs on Joey out the corner of my eye. "What?"

"Soylent Green is people." Scout indicates the closest red pods. They're made of glass or thick plastic but the surface is covered with frost. But, yeah. People, person, shaped thing inside.

There's movement in the distance behind Joey. I look over my shoulder. The Gate is still there. I look forward. A cluster of guys dressed in black coming up behind Joey, knives in hand.

More Legion to reinforce—I blink, not quite believing what I'm seeing.

Some of them don't have their faces covered and they're all Joey.

I hear a squeaking noise. Scout is rubbing the frost off the glass of one of the red pods.

The Legions are with Joey now. A dozen Joeys. Frak me.

Enough is enough. "We gotta go, Scout."

"You need to see this."

I take a couple of steps toward her. She's cleared away a six-inch circle. A girl is inside.

It's me.

New Delhi, 31 October 1984 A.D.

"You will all die if you let her do this!" Neeley cried out.

All activity in the room paused for a moment, then went on as before.

Indira Gandhi walked over, shaking her head. "I truly would like to know who you are. Where you come from. I think that would be an intriguing story. But you are nothing. Nobody. I was giving you the gift of dawn and history, but you have rejected that."

She signaled and the two Sikh guards came over.

"Take her outside and execute her."

The two men exchanged glances, then the senior of the two nodded. "Yes, Prime Minister."

Neeley prepared to fight as soon as they cut her loose.

Which was fruitless as they lifted Neeley, still tied to the chair, and carried her between them. Out of the door, into a garden behind the house. She recognized the place.

Neeley struggled, jerking back and forth to no avail. They set the chair down and took a couple of steps away from her. One was armed with a Sterling submachinegun and the other drew a revolver from a shoulder holster.

"Hold on!" Neeley said. She'd stopped struggling because she didn't want to tip the chair over and die lying on the ground. This was bad enough. "Do you know what she's doing? She's going to nuke Pakistan. Karachi, Hyderabad, and Islamabad. Millions are going to die. Why? You're not at war!"

The two once more exchanged looks, but the one with the sub raised it to his shoulder, aiming at her.

"Satwant Singh," Neeley said. "Why do you serve a ruler who sent troops into the Golden Temple? Who has been killing your people?" She looked at the man with the revolver. "Beant Singh. Why are you doing the same?"

The barrel of the submachinegun dropped slightly. "How do you know our names?" Satwant demanded.

"I know if the Prime Minister is not stopped millions will die today. And it will not end there. The Chinese will get involved. The Russians. The Americans. A fire will be ignited. Here." Neeley nodded her head toward the residence. "A fire that will consume the planet."

Satwant lowered the Sterling. "Who are you?"

Neeley looked to the east. The slightest tint of gray in the dark sky. BMNT was quickly approaching. She remembered Gant teaching her the term: beginning morning nautical twilight. *When the bad guys attack.* She didn't know what dawn was for Gandhi. BMNT? Sunrise?

Her arrival had made it worse, Neeley realized. The Shadow had played this perfectly, telling Gandhi just enough to set this up.

"What do you think she will do to your people now, if she's willing to kill millions of Pakistanis? Who will stop her? What will stop her?"

According to history, these two assassinated Gandhi at 9:20 this morning. Surely that hadn't been a spur of the moment decision? The download indicated it hadn't been.

"You were going to kill her anyway," Neeley said. "This morning."

Beant turned to his partner. "How does she know this?"

"Why don't you kill her before she kills millions?" Neeley suggested. It was lighter in the east.

"We should run," Satwant said to his comrade. "Get away."

Beant shook his head. "It is too late. She is right. We must—"

"What are you doing?" Gandhi came forward, along the garden path, passing through the wicket gate.

To the spot where history—

Beant fired three times in rapid succession, the bullets striking the Prime Minister in the stomach. She staggered back, hands clasped over her abdomen. "Oh!" she exclaimed. "No. It can't be. Not now. It's too soon."

She went to her knees.

Satwant fired the Sterling on automatic, the 9 mm bullets hitting her as she held her hands up in an instinctive protective gesture.

She was blown backward by the impacts.

Satwant's submachinegun stopped firing, the bolt locked back, the magazine empty.

Guards came rushing out of the house along with the Generals.

Both Sikhs threw their weapons to the ground and raised their hands to surrender. Both were gunned down in blaze of fire from several guards. Several rounds passed close by Neeley.

A man knelt next to Gandhi, checking her. Several of the Generals were shouting orders.

One of the security guards ran up to Neeley and pointed his submachinegun at her head, his finger twitching on the trigger.

North Atlantic, 31 October 1941 A.D.

"You open the outside hatch and escape," Topp said to Roland. "We are not very deep. You can make it to the surface. Perhaps the other escort ships will find you. They will be quartering the water for survivors."

Roland turned to Jager and relayed the plan.

"Yes," Jager said. "I will help the Captain open the hatch once you flood the compartment. We must be quick. I do not have much more time"

Topp was already at the forward hatch. "I am ready. You must make sure you tie yourself off to the rung just inside the top hatch so you are not swept back in here. You are a strong man and we are not very deep. You will be able to open it against the water pressure. Once the first surge is past, get out. Then there will be a second surge when you open the way to the engine room."

Roland had never cared for the Navy, but he had to admit their Captains could make decisions swiftly and decisively. He nodded. "I will get the outside hatch. I—" he wasn't certain what else to say.

Jager put a hand on Roland's shoulder. "Good hunting."

Roland nodded. "The same. Your name will be revered in your lodge."

Jager crawled forward, next to Topp. He indicated for Roland to go up.

Roland reached up, gripping the edge of the inside lip of the loading hatch and pulled himself up, into the narrow tube.

"Do it!" Topp's voice carried the edge of command, echoing up to Roland.

Roland tied his belt off to the rung, looping it under both his arms. Then he grabbed the wheel.

"I hate the water," he muttered. He took several deep breaths.

Then he turned the wheel. It spun easily enough, *well-maintained*, Roland thought. Then it came to a stop. Getting as much leverage as he could, Roland pushed upward. Nothing for a moment, then water began to seep in. He pushed harder. The hatch popped open and the sea surged in.

Roland was slammed back against the side of the tube, the belt keeping him from being sucked back inside.

It only took a few seconds, then all was still. Roland was floating, the room below him flooded. He unbuckled the belt, push up, out of the tube. Into a forest of kraken tentacles waving about.

He slashed as one came at him. There was daylight above.

He looked down. No second surge of water.

Another tentacle attacked and Roland barely dodged it.

Still nothing from below.

Roland reached down and pulled himself back into the hatch, along the tube, into the torpedo room.

The red emergency lights were still on, German engineering. Topp and Jager were struggling with the hatch. Topp had his feet on the bulkhead, using his thigh muscles to pull, his hands on the wheel.

Jager was unwrapping the tourniquet for some reason. As Roland swam closer he saw why; Jager jammed the wrench as a lever, trying to help Topp. Blood pulsed out of his limb.

But the hatch wasn't moving.

Roland fought the panic of being trapped, underwater, carbon dioxide beginning to burn his lungs. He focused on the hatch. He swam next to Topp, reached down, his hands next to the Germans. He put his feet on the bulkhead and squatted.

All those years in the weight rooms, lifting sandbags during deployments, all that work was coming down to this one moment.

Roland began to lift.

Out of the corner of his eye he could see a kraken tentacle blindly come through the torpedo loading tube, blindly searching. Jager let go of the wrench, floating, motionless.

Roland closed his eyes and put it all into one effort.

The hatch popped open and Roland, Topp and Jager were swept into the engine room, flooding it.

Roland hit something, machinery, then something else, covered in scales, a Grendel. His lungs were screaming, stars exploding in his brain from lack of oxygen.

I hate the water.

The Multiverse

Scout rubbed a clear circle on the glass of the other red pod. A young man was inside, like the girl who looked like Lara, floating inside.

"Lukas," Lara whispered, standing at her side.

Scout checked out the threat. A dozen Legion were spreading out, moving to encircle them. They were in no rush, confident in their numbers. The Gate, a black, shimmering rectangle, was still open and the path to it clear.

"Okay," Scout said. "Time to get."

Lara didn't move. She had a hand on the cold glass, peering at the person inside.

Scout grabbed Lara's shoulder and pulled her away from the pod. "We've *got* to go."

Dazed, Lara nodded.

Scout forced her toward the Gate, noting that the Legion were charging. She shoved Lara as hard she could without knocking her over. They ran and Lara was snatched into the darkness. As Scout was about to enter she took one last look.

At this angle she could see out one of the tall windows on the side of the building.

"Frak me!" she exclaimed upon the sight outside that was revealed and then she was into the Gate.

The Return

IVAR sat on the Lexington Avenue subway, sandwiched between Angus and Edith. "Where are we going?"

"The Possibility Palace," Edith said.

Angus was covered in dust, but it was New York City. He could have been covered in purple paint and no one would have cared.

"How do we get there?" Ivar said. "Legion wanted to know that, but I couldn't tell him. Why couldn't I tell him?"

"Because I blocked it in your memory," Edith said.

"Oh. Okay."

Edith glanced past him at Angus. "How come there weren't police and fire racing there if you set off those charges? I didn't see anything from outside."

"I imploded everything inside the floor," Angus said. "A dust initiator charge. I'd tell you how to rig one, but you don't be wanting such information clouding up your pretty mind."

"Right," Edith said.

"They'll be there soon enough," Angus said, "but the building's fine. Everything on that floor though, isn't."

The train pulled into a station and the conductor's voice was garbled. "86th Street. 86th Street."

"Our stop," Edith announced.

The three stood.

"It will be a ripple," Ivar said. "All those servers gone."

"It's not a ripple," Edith said. "It's part of our present."

The doors slide open and they stepped onto the platform.

167

"Oh, yes," Angus said. He pulled a phone out of his pocket. "Thank you for letting me use this."

Edith took her phone back. She noticed that the counter was stopped at 00:18.

Angus smiled. "Plenty of time, lass. Plenty of time."

*****

EAGLE was above the Valley of Death, not sure if he were dead or alive. He looked at his hands and they were unmarked from the electricity that had gone through him into the watering hole.

He looked down from a vantage point a hundred meters up. Bodies of 'baby' Grendels floated on top of the water. So many, one couldn't even see any water. Just dead monsters.

The last of the Grendels were going down as the 'loins' of Shaka Zulu's army attacked.

The last thing he saw was Jager, bleeding from a half-dozen wounds, battling the final Aglaeca.

*****

DEATH wasn't so bad, Roland thought as he floated in a black ether of nothingness. His lungs didn't hurt any more. And he wasn't in water. But his clothes were wet. Did one have clothes in heaven?

He smiled, thinking of what Neeley would say to that. Hell was a more likely destination for him.

But there was light, growing brighter. He was in the air. Above the water and he knew. He was going back. But for now he was above the North Atlantic. He looked down. He could see the dark cigar shape of the U-Boat just below the surface, surrounded by kraken. But then it began to fade, going down.

The kraken were wrapping their tentacles around it, trying to keep it up, as their internal 'jets' blew water, trying to swim with the ship.

Didn't think of that, Roland realized.

There was a popping noise as an interior hatch gave way.

Not going to work bitches, Roland thought to himself. The U-boat was going down, taking the kraken with it.

168

And Captain Topp and his crew. And Jager. And the Grendel and Aglaeca and Legion and the eggs.

To join the *Reuben James*. In the darkness at the bottom of the ocean.

Roland flashed forward, back to his time.

Tell me, what were their names, tell me what were their names?

Did you have a good friend on the Reuben James?

*****

NEELEY was in the tunnel of time, trying to understand.

Anything.

How had an assassination almost turned into Armageddon?

Her hands were throbbing, the burns on her body pulsed with pain.

She didn't care. She wrapped her arms around herself allowing herself to be carried back.

She saw a timeline to one side. Those cities Gandhi had targeted in Pakistan blossoming with the bright flash of nuclear bursts.

It didn't happen, Neeley thought.

Or did it?

And then she was back and Roland was draping a blanket over her, gathering her in his powerful arms. "What did they do to you?" he asked, his eyes wide with concern.

Neeley managed a smile. "How was your trip, dear?"

"I drowned," Roland said, "but I'm better now. Let me take care of you."

*****

LARA saw Unity Hale wandering through the forest. The girl wasn't afraid, stopping every so often to examine a plant. Occasionally she gathered leaves or dug out a root, putting it in a makeshift pouch slung over one shoulder.

Lara felt the pull back to her own time, but fought against it, worried about the girl who wasn't worried about herself.

Frak me.

A half-dozen Native Americans leapt out of hiding positions and surrounded Unity, knives and hatchets raised.

Unity smiled at them and waved. She held up the pouch. She twirled and danced and acted like a complete lunatic in Lara's eyes.

The surrounding warriors lowered their weapons.

One of the Native Americans came forward. Lara stopped dancing and held out the bag. He looked in it and nodded. Then issued orders. The others turned and headed off. He looked at Unity. He smiled, nodded and indicated for her to follow.

The tribe had a new medicine woman.

Unity was fine and Lara was snatched back to her time.

But she remembered the people in the red pods and screamed into the ether of time.

*****

SCOUT allowed herself to be borne forward, sideways, whatever way she was coming from whenever and wherever she'd been, without much awareness. There was no sign of Lara and the Gate had not led back to the house and kitchen.

All Scout could think of was what she'd seen outside of that window: The massive golden tower at the center of Atlantis, reaching up into the sky, and above it, a massive dome extending out of sight in all directions. The dome had been dirty and smeared and the sky outside dark, with blood red streaks in filthy clouds.

Scout finally noticed that Lachesis was at her side, moving through the time tunnel with her.

"That was the Shadow's world," Scout said.

"It was," Lachesis confirmed.

"When was that? When in the past?"

"It wasn't the past," Lachesis said. "That was the Shadow timeline. Now."

The End
For Now

Our History Afterward

Zero Day-Zero Year

Zero Day vulnerabilities are considered precious in the eyes of hackers; and nations, whose security agencies accumulate them for possible exploits. At the very start of ARPANET, even before the first Internet message sent on Black Tuesday, 1969, Willis Ware warned about the inevitable in a classified paper that, in essence, stated that once you put information on a computer network you're creating inherent vulnerabilities—there would be no more secrets.

Willis Ware was a consultant on a 1983 movie, *War Games*. At a meeting of the National Security Council, Ronald Reagan, who'd watched the movie the previous weekend at Camp David, asked, out of the blue, if anyone else had seen the movie? No one had since it had just come out. Reagan begins to describe the movie and everyone in the room is exchanging glances like: "What's he talking about?" Reagan then tasked the Chairman of Joint Chiefs to report back to him on whether the scenario in the movie, where a kid hacks into the nuclear launch system, was possible. The next week, the Chairman reported back to Reagan that not only was it possible, the entire situation was much worse and "Our computer systems are vulnerable to electronic interference and interception by foreign powers, by criminals."

We really haven't gotten much better.

Zululand, Africa, 31 October 1828 A.D.

Because there is no first hand account of Shaka Zulu's life and reign, the stories often conflict. He did revolutionize warfare in South Africa and built a kingdom that lasted for over fifty years.

Shaka was assassinated by his half-brother, Dingane and two others in 1828. One of Dingane's first acts was to kill all of his family who might threaten him for the throne. Except for a half-brother,

Mpande who was considered too weak to be a threat. Naturally, Mpande eventually assassinated Dingane and took the throne.

In 1879, the Zulus dealt the British their greatest defeat in Africa at Isandlwana. It was a Pyrrhic victory though as the British increased their forces and wreaked vengeance, essentially ending the Zulu Kingdon.

Salem Massachusetts, 31 October 1692 A.D.

Salem, MA was settled in 1629 and named Salem, for Shalom, a Hebrew word meaning 'place of peace'.

The first accusations of witchcraft occurred in January 1692. As the year went accusations and counter-accusations flew. The first hanging occurred on 10 June. All told 19 people are hanged. One, Giles Corey, was pressed to death because he refused to confess, because that would allow the states to seize all his property from his family. He last words were "More weight."

New Delhi, 31 October 1984 A.D.

After Indira Gandhi's assassination, over 3,000 Sikhs were killed in riots, much of it state-sponsored and sanctioned. Her son. Rajiv, stated in an interview: "When a big tree falls, the earth shakes."

Her legacy is mixed, with some viewing her as a messiah who helped the poor while others view her as a power-hungry manipulator. She instigated the "Emergency" when many rights were pulled. She did bring Bangladesh into existence after leading India to victory in a war with Pakistan. She also made India a nuclear power.

Over 10,000 people a day visit the garden where she was assassinated.

North Atlantic, 31 October 1941 A.D.

The sinking of the *Reuben James* exacerbated already tense relations with Germany; however, not to the extent that war was declared. That would happen a little over five weeks later after the Japanese bombed Pearl Harbor.

Germany refused to apologize for the sinking, insisting the ship was operating in a war zone. The sinking did lead to the Coast Guard being moved from a peace-time role as part of the Treasury Department to becoming part of the US Navy. Congress also amended the Neutrality Act, allowing merchant ships to be armed and allowing them to enter European waters.

The Navy named a Fletcher-class destroyer the *USS Heywood L. Edwards*. The ship served in the Pacific theater throughout World War II. In the odd twists of the way of the world, the *USS Heywood L. Edwards* ended up being given to the Japanese Defense Forces to serve in their navy after the war. It was scrapped in 1976.

Wittenberg, Germany, 31 October 1517 A.D.

While it is commonly accepted as truth, the story of Martin Luther nailing his 95 theses to the door of All Saints Church in Wittenberg is perhaps more legend than true. We do know he did send the theses to his Bishop, Albert of Mainz. The theses were translated from Latin to German in January 1518 and were then printed and widely disseminated throughout Europe.

About Bob Mayer

Bob Mayer is a New York Times bestselling author, a graduate of West Point, former Special Operations, and the feeder of two yellow Labs, most famously Cool Gus. He's had over seventy books published, including the #1 bestselling series Area 51, Atlantis, and the Green Berets. Born in the Bronx and having traveled the world (usually not the tourist spots), he now lives peacefully with his wife and his Labs.

He has a free Reader's Guide listing all books with information about them here on Amazon. He also has free eBooks, short stories and audiobooks on his web site www.bobmayer.com He wrote under a number of pen names including Robert Doherty (Area 51) and Greg Donegan (Atlantis)

For more check: www.bobmayer.com

Printed in Great Britain
by Amazon